"We've got a situation here, sir!" a bus guard shouted into the CB radio. "The plane has been taken over! Repeat! The plane has been taken over!"

Before he finished the message, airport security men were grabbing flak jackets and shotguns and M-16s and racing out to emergency vans. Within seconds, vans were squealing into turns, heading out on the tarmac.

In the U.S. Marshal car still remaining next to the C-123, Starky received the news over his radio.

"Those guards ain't guards," said the voice of the BOP man in the control center. "They're cons. Stall 'em."

"Christ," Starkey responded. "How we supposed to do that?"

"You gotta come up with something. You gotta do something bold. But watch your ass."

"Yeah, sure. Go out there to those lifers and stall 'em, and watch my ass."

CON AIR

a novel by
RICHARD WOODLEY

based on the screenplay by
SCOTT ROSENBERG

Mandarin

Published in the United Kingdom in 1997 by
Mandarin Paperbacks

1 3 5 7 9 10 8 6 4 2

Copyright © Disney Enterprises, Inc. 1997
Photo insert copyright © Touchstone Pictures
Photos by Frank Masi

This book is sold subject to the condition that it shall not,
by way of trade or otherwise, be lent, resold, hired out,
or otherwise circulated without the publisher's prior consent
in any form of binding or cover other than that in which it is
published and without a similar condition including this
condition being imposed on the subsequent purchaser

Mandarin Paperbacks
Random House UK Limited
20 Vauxhall Bridge Road, London SW1V 2SA

Random House Australia (Pty) Limited
20 Alfred Street, Milsons Point, Sydney
New South Wales 2061, Australia

Random House New Zealand Limited
18 Poland Road, Glenfield, Auckland 10, New Zealand

Random House South Africa (Pty) Limited
Endulini, 5a Jubilee Road, Parktown 2193, South Africa

Random House UK Limited Reg. No. 954009

A CIP catalogue record for this book
is available from the British Library

Papers used by Random House UK Limited
are natural, recyclable products made from wood grown in
sustainable forests. The manufacturing processes conform to
the environmental regulations of the country of origin

Printed and bound in Great Britain by
Cox & Wyman Ltd, Reading, Berkshire

ISBN 0 7493 3690 0

"The degree of civilization in a society can be judged by observing its prisoners . . ."

Fyodor Dostoyevsky

CON
AIR

ONE

From the bow of the tugboat, the dark line of the shore seemed like a sprawling base for tongues of fire and bellows of smoke. The huge pipes of refineries snaked through the gloom, huge Erector-set derricks bobbed, all limned by the fires from the towering burn stacks.

Cameron Poe stood alone at the bow in the misty sea breeze and wondered whether he was looking at his future or his past. He was relieved to salute his thanks to the helmsman and step off the tug in port. He hauled his duffel down the gangplank and out to the highway where he could thumb a ride down the coast away from the fire and smoke.

· · · ·

"Well, soldier, at least you're home now."

"Yeah, Vernon." Cameron Poe breathed deep of
the damp air blowing past the window of the rat-
tling Dodge pickup. "And at least it ain't dry as last
year's pig poop."

"No, no it ain't. Marina's coming up, mile or
so, be there on the left."

Cameron Poe was just starting to relax. But it
would take a while to flush the sand out of his system. The sand that still crept into his eyes and ears
and up his ass in his dreams; that waited still in
his deep pockets to grit up his fingernails and his
handkerchief every time he wanted to blow his
nose; the sand that clouded his vision like a rasping
fog and through which, in his dreams, he still saw
men blown apart in air so dry it seemed to suck the
blood away before arms and legs flopped back to
the desert floor. In his dreams, he saw the earth as
if he were an eagle, and saw the ground suddenly
hurtle up to meet him too fast. In his dreams, bullets pierced his black beret and leeches squirmed
inside his jump boots.

"So, captain, you got plans?"

"Pardon?"

"Your chest shows a lot of experience, all those
medals and ribbons. Prolly all over the world, huh?
Paratroop wings. Ranger, huh? Nifty outfit, the
beret and all. Been shot at? Desert Storm? Young as

you are, you got some big plans to come home on? You got plans for tonight, say?"

The grizzled farmer in the floppy hat had accommodated Poe this evening through all these Alabama miles by keeping relatively quiet and not asking questions. They had introduced themselves and passed occasional pleasantries. It was as if now, just before splitting safely away, the man could risk the probing he had so far resisted.

"Just gonna relax some." Tiny drops blew in the window and spattered his face, and he smelled the Gulf. He wanted to savor the old memories from long ago that wafted in on the southern breeze and flood out the newer, more recent ones. Never again would he crawl on his belly or darken his face with paint or hang from a rope or drop from a plane; he wanted no more of those silent, superhot adrenaline rushes followed by gurgles of blood and bodies in front of him; never again would he strap on a killing knife above his ankle or carry a length of piano wire with which you could sever a head. His left shoulder would always ache from tissue torn by a 7.62-millimeter bullet, his left knee would always stiffen in damp weather, like now, from too many hard landings in dark places. No more ambushes. No more explosions. No more dread. He craved a peaceful time to heal his wounded dreams. From now on, he wanted everything open and clear and harmless. For a while, he didn't want to plan anything at all. He was bone tired and excited at the same time. He was almost home, almost safe.

"Well, here we are, Mr. Poe, Captain Poe."

"Mister's fine. Much obliged for the lift, Vernon. You take care, now."

"You bet. And thanks for everything you done for the country, whatever."

Cameron Poe stepped out into the drizzle, swung the door shut, reached under the tarp in the bed and hauled out his duffel, then tapped on the window to signal his completion and waved. He watched the pickup lights disappear in the mist around the bend.

Cameron Poe breathed deep of the damp air, savoring the hint of kudzu that wafted off the unseen vines, and thought that it had been a long time—it seemed like years when it was only days—since he had been mustered out of the U.S. Army Rangers, free to be peaceful for the first time in seven long years. More than anything he wanted peace. And somewhere in that, second or third, he wanted to put together a hot car and drive faster than he'd ever driven before.

It had not been peaceful, ever, for Cameron Poe. He dropped out of high school in Montgomery not so much to join the army as to get away from home. Home was a grandmother who took care of him because his mother wouldn't, and a father who came around only to reek of alcohol and slug him for one thing or another. When came that day that Cameron slugged him back, his father vowed to kill him one day soon, and that seemed as good a time as any for Cameron to cut the traces. He went into the army looking for somebody to hit. Nothing was tough enough for him. He wanted the toughest of the toughest. Airborne looked good. But the Rangers were even tougher. They did everything. They parachute jumped, they climbed, they rappelled, they swam. Special-action missions, pathfinders, raiders, commandos. First into a spot, first out. You found something. You blew something up. You secured something. You got somebody out. Gung-ho teamwork, but on your own at the same time. Fall on your sword if the time came. You wore the black beret and that black-and-yellow shoulder patch that said "Rangers" and you didn't have to say anything else. Which was just fine with Cameron Poe, because if he had his druthers he'd hardly say anything at all.

His grandmother died when he was slogging through Fort Benning boonies in recon training, and he'd never been home since. Not to that home, anyway.

A huge facsimile of the Ranger coat of arms hung on a blue curtain at the back of the hall on discharge day: the lion with its raised paw, the tomahawk and powder horn, the slogan "Rangers Lead The Way."

Colonel Brack strutted back and forth before a group of stern-faced Rangers at attention, tapping his swagger stick into his palm.

"Army Rangers have a proud history," he intoned, his thick eyebrows wiggling up and down. "Since the French and Indian War in 1756, Rangers have been leading the way in every major confrontation in which the United States has been involved."

Cameron Poe's mind drifted. Some of those seven long years had been bitter. He shouldn't have slugged the sergeant, but what the hell, it took too much time to explain some things to some people. It had set him back a little. And also he lost a little faith in the brass who seemed to weasel around with the episode, trying to figure out a way to pretend that nothing had happened. Cameron Poe would have taken his medicine. Instead he had to make an off-the-record apology. He hated to apologize. Put him in a cell, fine. Don't make him say he was sorry.

". . . And you men are a credit to this fine heritage, and I am sorry to see you go. But you have served your country well and displayed the intestinal fortitude required to fight on to the Ranger objective and complete the mission . . ."

Cameron Poe thought: "Intestinal fortitude" hell. You got the job done, that's all. That's the trouble with talk.

". . . and never leaving a fallen comrade behind, regardless of the odds or the enemy . . ."

What the hell; the enemy *was* the odds. And the enemy was everywhere. Never trust anybody, that was Cameron Poe's attitude. Give me a job and step aside. Don't promise me anything, and I won't promise you. That's just words. Tell me what you want done. If I can't do it, I'll tell you. That hasn't happened yet.

". . . I thank you. America thanks you. Good luck in wherever you may go. And remember: Rangers lead the way!"

Cameron Poe never forgot anything.

Off across the highway, down among the docks a hundred yards away and lit by one of four mercury vapor lamps that gave everything a cold, raw glow, he saw moored a somewhat seedy white 100-foot boat with a refurbished large square superstructure with porthole windows gleaming orange like jack-o'-lanterns—clearly a yacht converted to a bar or a party boat. It was his nature now to have a flash of competency: He recognized in a moment just how he could sneak up to that craft; how he could board it and overpower guards; how he could blow it up; how he could remove a hostage; or how he could just approach like a wraith to assess the situation in crucial detail and withdraw without ever having been seen. These fleeting mental scenarios afflicted him no matter how much he hated them or how much he resisted them; these were now the irrelevant workings of his trained mind.

He lit a cigarette and pulled a small piece of paper out of his left breast pocket. By the flickering match he read again what was handwritten on it: "Pier 39. Come alone." He flicked the match off into a puddle and took a couple of deep drags as he replaced the paper in his pocket and eyed the boat. He finished the cigarette and flicked it away as he had the match, bent down to brush off any possible ashes from his sharply creased trousers neatly bloused and tucked into his glistening boots, hoisted his duffel to his shoulder, and ambled across the empty highway toward the boat.

From the gangplank he could see through a porthole window that it was in fact a bar. He heard canned rock music. There was a scattering of tables and a lot of grubby customers at the tables and the bar, men who might have been fishermen or dockworkers, and two waitresses. The one closest to the window was waiting for the bartender to pour four shots of Wild Turkey. She was about twenty-five, with a short, sturdy, athletic body, dark hair in a pixie cut, and a lopsided smile that caused Cameron Poe himself to smile for the first time that day.

He entered the bar casually, put down his duffel, strode across the floor, and spun the woman around into a hug. He kissed her hard on the mouth and then said, "How's my baby?"

"Damn, Poe, you finally did come. Which one?"

"Both."

"I'm fine, you big lug. The other is—whoa!"

He had dropped to his knees and leaned his ear to her belly.

"You aren't gonna hear anything yet, Poe. I'm only a couple of months along."

"You'd be surprised what I hear, Tricia Poe. I lean on you, I can hear the day we were married, I can hear what you been up to, I can hear our baby."

"I been up to saving a few dollars and counting off the days and then the hours until you got here."

"You could have told me what it was."

"You wouldn't have liked me working here. You knew it was me, with that note, don't lie."

"I figured maybe it was."

"Who else is all of a sudden gonna tell you to

come to some dock and come alone? And if you didn't know who, you wouldn't of come. I know you, Cameron Poe."

"Well, ain't that just fine, being that you're my wife."

"Go sit. I gotta work a bit." She glanced at the door. "Shit."

Three men had come in, and heads turned at the noise of their heavy cowboy boots and then turned away at the quick recognition of the uncommon trio. Even in this rough-hewn place, these men were obviously special. People stepped aside to allow a path for them to stomp to the bar. "Billy Joe, Smoke, Ronnie," the bartender nodded deferentially, wiping the surface in front of them while they together turned and leaned back against the bar and scanned the room.

They were similar to each other, bearded and burly, unkempt and red-eyed, the most apparent difference being Billy Joe's greasy ponytail.

"Hey there, Tricia," Billy Joe called out while the other two grunted. "Whyn't y'all join us for a short one."

"No thanks," Tricia said, as Cameron sat down at a table.

"Come on, now."

"You know these huckleberries?" Cameron asked.

"They're regulars," she answered more softly.

"Who's a huckleberry?" Smoke rumbled. "You one, Billy Joe?"

"Shit no."

"We're regulars, all right," Smoke said, "regular hound dogs!"

"Don't bother with it, Cameron," Tricia said softly, tapping his shoulder.

"Hey, soldier boy," Billy Joe called, "whyn't you buy us nice fellows a round on gummint money?"

"It's nothing, Cameron," Tricia said.

Billy Joe wadded some bills into a small ball and threw them at Poe. The wad hit his face lightly and fluttered down.

"Case you ain't got gummint money, boy, use some a that," Billy Joe said, leaning back against the bar and crossing his feet. "Haw! Then maybe we all can play a few little night games with the little kitty there."

"We don't need trouble," Tricia whispered into his ear. "Come on, Daddy, let's dance. A little John Cougar'll calm you down."

She pulled him up from the table and they began a sedate two-step just to keep moving. They felt eyes on them. She felt his arms relax a little.

"For a minute there, you were that guy again."

"Yeah."

"He ain't supposed to come around anymore."

"Nope."

"It's peacetime, Cameron Poe. You're home now. Just another private man. Family man, at that."

"Yup."

Suddenly Billy Joe was at his shoulder, offering a belch. "Ho, soldier boy, I guess I'll just cut in."

Tricia tensed, but Cameron did not. "No, mister. This is a special occasion, so I'll just spend it dancing with my wife."

"I don't remember askin' you, soldier boy, 'cause you just another jarhead ridin' the taxpayers' dick."

Tricia tried to steer them away, angling toward the bar.

"Nice hat, huckleberry!" Smoke guffawed across the floor.

Cameron removed his beret and rolled it up in his hand.

"Plus, it pisses me off you gettin' the only decent piece of beaver left in the county."

Billy Joe reached for Tricia's arm, and she brushed him off, at the same time saying, "No, Poe, no."

But Cameron Poe had already reacted, and when Billy Joe's hand touched Tricia's belly, Cameron yanked him by the back of the collar, then lifted him with both arms and tossed him against the bar. The bartender dropped out of sight.

Billy Joe bounced off the bar and fell onto a table, spilling beer and scattering customers.

Smoke and Ronnie charged, swinging wildly, connecting a couple of times before Cameron kicked Smoke's feet out from under him and dropped Ronnie with two short uppercuts. Smoke clambered back to his feet and got his nose broken by Cameron's straight right and his breath taken away by a chop to his diaphragm. Another chop to the back of his neck ended Smoke's night in a bleeding heap on the floor.

Billy Joe launched himself back into it, swinging a leg from the table he had crunched, immediately finding his right knee collapsed by Poe's kick and his knuckles smashed against the floor when Poe stomped on the club in his hand. He raised himself with the help of Poe hauling him up by the ponytail, and then Poe smacked both his ears with his palms and left him reeling in pain until he slumped in a corner.

Oblivious as always to the hubbub around him and focused only on the job at hand—which had been first to disable the enemy defensively and now was to withdraw—Poe grabbed Tricia's elbow as she daubed at a two-inch gash over his eye with a napkin, and hurried toward the door.

Rain pelted them and lightning competed with the flames of the far-off stacks. Through the door behind them charged Billy Joe, out of kilter but rabid, and the lightning flashed on the blade of his Buck knife as he took a vicious swipe at Poe's back, slicing his jacket, shirt, and short ribs.

As Poe swung around, Billy Joe planted his feet unsteadily and taunted him, weaving the blade in the air. "Let's go, huckleberry horseshit, come ahead on!"

Poe's first kick sent the knife spinning off the dock. A straight, sharp thrust of his rigid knuckles cracked Billy Joe's sternum. As Billy Joe's head snapped forward from that blow, the heel of Poe's left hand drove his nose bone up into his brain.

Poe watched Billy Joe sink onto the dock and drew deep breaths to regain his own equilibrium and rid himself of the awful, blind ferocity that took him over sometimes. He heard Tricia sobbing a few yards away.

The boat door opened again as Ronnie lurched out, stopped in confusion, then dropped to his knees beside the crumpled form of Billy Joe. He put a hand to the carotid artery under his jaw. "You killed him!" Ronnie howled. "You fucking killed Billy Joe!"

Cameron Poe reached into his trouser pocket and took out a quarter. He walked over to the phone mounted on the light pole and dialed 911. But the wail of sirens already reached him from a narrowing distance.

TWO

It was over just so quickly—the mission, the engagement, the flight, the freedom. He had traveled so far in a day, had experienced so much. Yet Cameron Poe sat on a cot and avoided contemplation about what had happened. Done was done. What lay ahead was not entirely in his control. His job now was to focus on what he could control. No physical action was required or apt. First, he had decisions to make. A mental exercise, a matter of logic, of disciplined thought.

He recounted for the man sitting on the opposite cot quite precisely what had happened. The man recounted to him a story at crucial variance with Poe's account.

"They are saying," the man said, "that you disabled Billy Joe Hubbard and that while he was at your mercy you beat him to death."

The man had come to the cell at the county jail unshaven and unhappy with his Friday night being interrupted, and had announced that he was Robert Liebreich, a public defender assigned to represent Cameron Poe.

"I ain't a rocket scientist," Liebreich had proclaimed, "but I know the law. And you got the word of three known locals against your own, and you ain't lived here steady for seven years. You got the skills to kill a man. So one thing you could do is let me plea bargain, admit you were drunk and out of your frigging mind."

"The man came at me with a knife. I wasn't drunk."

"Well, *he* was, and that ain't necessarily any better for you, if they can argue that the man was too drunk to defend himself."

"They're lying."

"They can't find the knife, Mr. Poe. If it went in the drink where you say, the storm current must have swirled it out of there." He waited, but Cameron Poe said nothing, just fixed him with his blue eyes, seldom blinking. "You could get ten years. You take a plea, admit it, you get maybe four, serve maybe a year." He waited, Poe said nothing. "Listen, before you consulted with me, unfortunately you admitted the man was already disarmed when you struck the fatal blow." He waited. "Listen,

your wife's with child, my friend. At this time, in
this county, you're up shit's crick, 'cause they will
look out for their own. My advice to you, sir, is,
serve a few months, put it behind you, watch your
child grow up."

For some reason, Cameron Poe's thoughts
flashed on his father, and for some reason that
made him more sad than angry. There was a certain
self-righteous quality to his attitudes, central to
which was his belief that he never went looking for
trouble, never ran from danger or threat, never lied
to himself, and never denied reality. He'd fought
and killed for this country, no problem. And now
he'd fought and killed for himself, and look where
he was. Reality was screwy, but there it was. When
they'd slapped the cuffs on him, Tricia had tried to
scratch the cop's eyes out.

"Okay," he said.

Judge Minerva Tift looked over her glasses, which
were perched on the very end of her thick nose.
"Cameron Poe," she intoned, "you have pleaded
guilty to manslaughter in the first degree."

Cameron Poe thought he heard Tricia suck a
breath from the rear of the small courtroom.

". . . It is the order of this court that you be
remanded to the state penitentiary where you shall

remain incarcerated for a term not less than seven
to ten years."

"What?" Cameron whispered to his defender.
"*What?*"

Attorney Liebreich stared down at his table and
pursed his lips and shook his head.

"*What did she say?*"

"I'm sorry," Attorney Liebreich said. He tucked
his papers under his arm, rose, and walked away.

Deputies gently seized Cameron Poe under the
arms, raised him from his seat, cuffed him, and led
him toward a side door. When he glanced back,
Tricia was not crying, but she stood erect and
looked at him directly, clear-eyed, strong.

Cameron Poe was consigned to the top of three
tiers of cells. It was a world of steel and noise. The
cell doors clanked open and clanked shut, the catwalks seemed to carry the echoes. Inmates talked
and argued and occasionally screamed.

The first months were the easiest. Cameron Poe
knew discipline. And to a certain extent, the outside world for him seemed to remain frozen. Tricia
was just pregnant. She waited, he waited. He went
about his life mechanically, as if it weren't his life at
all. Within the walls, he was encysted, as if himself
unborn.

He survived by conforming to the imposed patterns of time and movement. Straight time, straight lines. The cell door clanked open, he walked to the mess hall. He finished eating, he walked straight back. The cell door clanked open, he walked straight to the yard. He ran a few laps on the track, lifted some weights, and walked straight back to the cell. Every hour of every day was accounted for, assigned its route and task, and yet no hour or day was predictable. You did what you were supposed to do every hour or every day, an unvarying schedule. And yet anything could happen tomorrow. Anything could happen at any time.

By nature and training he was wary and watchful and tough. As he didn't concern himself with the past, he didn't concern himself with justice. Among his disciplines was the power to focus precisely on the job at hand. And the job at hand now was to survive—not just to stay alive, but to stay whole in mind and body. Your powers could be sapped in tiny increments; the way you stayed whole was to sustain your living ritual in the finest details. You stayed clean and clean-shaven, you walked erect, you kept your muscles toned, you exercised your mind.

He had the tremendous advantage of self-sufficiency. Nobody intimidated him. He didn't trust anybody. He didn't kowtow, didn't challenge any-

body, and because of his demeanor was seldom
challenged himself. He stayed within the rules,
written and unwritten. He didn't curry favor. He
didn't butter up the guards or the inmates. That
was how he sustained his dignity, and why he was
respected.

He didn't count the days. Days and hours were
not within his control. He monitored his own
strength and endurance, to stay ready always. That
was what he was trained to do.

It was hot in the cellblock. The air stank of prisoners.

"Hey, Slick," growled the big barrel-chested
man called Carp as they stood in the showers, when
Cameron Poe didn't respond to a question about
his sexual preferences. "I'm talking to you."

As others watched, Cameron Poe stepped out of
the shower and reached for a towel. He felt the
man's hand grab his wrist. With a quick, deft twist,
Poe broke the third metacarpal bone in the man's
hand.

"You're a dead man," said Carp, who stomped
away groaning and holding his hand.

. . .

Cameron Poe kept his prison-issued meal spoon in his pocket twenty-four, seven—twenty-four hours, seven days a week—as the rules prescribed. A second one, illegal, which he cadged from a former Green Beret working in the laundry, he kept hidden in a niche he carved out of the concrete floor under a leg of his cot. The handle of that one he had sharpened to a lethal-edged "shank," a necessary item of self-protection. On occasion, when he needed to be especially wary because of threats of trouble among various factions or gangs, or from disgruntled nuts that had to be avoided if possible, he kept that one with him, too, within the heel of his shoe.

He read his letters carefully and many times over. Tricia was feeling good, Tricia was lonely, Tricia was coping, Tricia loved him. Tricia, he said to himself over and over, Tricia. . . . He had decided not to have Tricia visit him. He decided to suspend the tantalizing agonies of such contact, so he could better steel himself for his everyday life without the distraction of something so disturbing as having your wife go through the metal detector and the search and the long walk between walls topped with silver razor wire to the visitors' center, where she would see him for two hours amid a hundred other prisoners.

He wrote letters. "Dear Tricia: I'm doing fine. Don't worry about a thing. Thanks for the broccoli. I ate it raw. The food's not bad. Don't worry about that. I did 200 pull-ups today, 50 more than yesterday, and said your name with every one. My shoulder's holding up. One of the guards beat up a little guy named Hernando yesterday, who knows why. Maybe the guy sassed him. Somebody's always getting whacked around, and somebody's always yelling someplace, but I keep my nose clean and don't cause trouble and they still leave me alone pretty much. I play cards sometimes with a small group of guys, gin or hearts. I'm reading quite a bit now. I read that Krishnamurti book out of the library, like you asked me to. I liked it pretty much. But you know me, I don't understand a lot of mumbo-jumbo. It's good to help pass the time anyway. Love and kisses, CP."

Tricia had a baby girl they had already decided to name Casey, since that could fit either boy or girl and was the name of Cameron Poe's father. He stared at the baby picture, memorizing every detail. Casey, he said to himself over and over, Casey. . . .

. . .

The guards walked the catwalks and sometimes banged on the cells with their clubs, for one reason or another. Cameron had learned not to jump at sudden noises. A guard banged on his cell bars and said, "Poe, come with me." Cameron walked ahead of the guard to the captain's office. "Yesterday when you were in the yard we found some contraband in your cell," the captain of the guards said. Cameron didn't ask what it was, didn't say anything. It was not necessary for him to speak. He just listened for the reason.

"Something's cooking between the Sabus and the Calicos," the captain said, referring to two of the major ethnic gangs on Cellblock B, his block. "Maybe you could help us there."

Both groups of blacks and Hispanics trusted Cameron Poe, or at least considered him safe. So the captain wanted him to turn snitch. That was the reason for finding the "contraband."

"No," Cameron Poe said.

"They already seen you walk down here," the captain said.

Cameron Poe had already given his answer. They escorted him to the warden's office. "Above all, we want peace in this institution," Warden Saar said. "You deserve a break. You could even save lives." After a silence, he said, "Those sugar packets are serious, but I'm quite willing to accept that they were an inadvertent mistake."

"Not *my* mistake," Cameron Poe said.

He was confined to his cell. With one of the meals delivered to him, he found a tiny note inside a square of cheese ravioli. "Your dead as a rat," the note said. Carp was a leader of the Calicos. One of his guys worked in the kitchen.

Poe opened a package from Tricia, or finished opening it, since it had already been inspected. A letter, two snapshots of Casey, two race-car magazines, four snowball cupcakes.

"Casey's third birthday," Tricia had written. "I know you felt bad about not being able to send anything, don't tell me different. Don't worry, it went fine. She had three little friends over. She told them her daddy was in the service, which I think she picked up from one of her friends who has a daddy in the navy and that's why he can't come home when he wants to."

He thumbed through the magazines while nibbling on a cupcake. "Hot out here," came a voice through the bars.

"Hey, Baby-O," Poe said to the man mopping the walkway.

"Gonna be hot," Baby-O Odell said softly, his young, unmarked face stern.

"Cake?"

"Don't mind if I do." Baby-O took the offered cupcake through the bars.

"Thanks," Poe said quietly, for the alert. Baby-O was a fringe member of the Sabus.

"Be glad you locked in," Baby-O said, chewing.

Poe leaned against the bars, listening.

"Won't be us niggers to watch out for," Baby-O said. "Be Carp."

Poe nodded.

Baby-O moved on, swabbing ahead of him.

There was a body in the yard. A black guy Poe didn't know. Somebody new. Side of his neck cut, from the base of the ear to the esophagus. Cons stayed away from it, didn't even look. Guards loaded it on a cart and wheeled it away. B Block was locked down.

Cameron Poe lay on his bunk staring into the darkness. It was too quiet in the block. An ordinary lockdown because somebody fucked up or mouthed off, that was one thing. Here, everybody was waiting.

The first night was quiet. The second night, after

midnight, there was a cry off down the block somewhere. Then there was breaking glass, a "whoosh."
Then hell broke loose.

Poe sprang to the bars, sticking out his metal
mirror to look right and left down the walkway.
There was hollering, sounds of running on catwalks, clanging on cell bars. There was a silent moment. Then alarms whined. Cell doors along the
block clanked open electronically all at once.
Flames danced on the walls. Cons flooded the catwalks and began to run. A torrent surged by his
open cell. He saw the quick blur of a length of pipe
too late and was knocked back against the rear wall
and sank to the floor.

Blood drizzled down over his ear, and he
couldn't focus his eyes. He felt along the floor to
the leg of his cot, lifted it, found the shank, palmed
it, tried and failed to struggle to his feet. There was
a crash of glass against his wall. Flames burst out all
around him. He couldn't see anything more than
swirling light, though he felt the heat.

A hand reached through a gap in the flames,
grabbed his shirt, pulled him forward. He reached
for the hand and seized it. Baby-O hauled him out
of the cell and dropped him on the catwalk.

"Come on, man, we gotta run!" Baby-O barked.

His clothes were singed, his head wobbled. He
began to focus. Baby-O was knocked over front-

ward, falling to his hands and knees. A hand grabbed Poe's singed hair and painfully yanked him upright. Carp stood before him with a guard's billy club raised. Poe dove blindly forward, his right hand extended, finding Carp's midsection just as the club thudded against his back. Carp sank slowly to the catwalk, groans mixed with bloody bubbles from his mouth.

Poe hurled the shank into a flaming adjacent cell not his own. He picked up Baby-O under his arms and hoisted him to his feet. They ran down the catwalk, away from the flames.

The melee between cons and guards was brief. It was an efficient prison; riot guns were in the guards' hands in what seemed like an instant. After a few broken heads, the horde of cons stopped their pell-mell rush and started backing up. Guards coming in the other way quickly extinguished the flames from the Molotov cocktails. There was only one death.

It was Cameron Poe's good luck that Baby-O accompanied him on the major transfer of cons to the federal penitentiary in California called San Quentin, because that meant that he had a friend in the new cellblock. The judgment back in Alabama had been that everybody on Cellblock B had participated in the "riot," and after the gang leaders were cited for punishment, nobody else was singled out. The transfer was not so much punishment for the transferees as a way to defuse the situation. Poe and the others received minor increases in their sentences. Authorities were unable to solve the murder of Hedrick "Giant Carp" Larry.

THREE

The letter Cameron Poe read aloud with such relish was written in red crayon. "My daddy is coming home on July 14," he read. "My birthday is July 14. I am going to see my daddy for the first time ever on July 14. I can't wait for July 14. Love, Casey."

"Makes me all mooshy inside," Baby-O said, chuckling. He licked the back of a yellow happy-face sticker and slapped it onto the cell wall over Poe's bunk. "You got good things waitin' for you, that's a true fact."

"You mocking me?"

"Hey, Poe, don't help me none mocking some-body about to go home." Baby-O laughed. "Just funny seeing you all revved up, face beaming like a lighthouse. What we been through together, man, make more sense you was mocking *me*. I'm stuck inside for a while yet, you know, someplace."

"Yeah." Poe slid a foot-long rectangular metal box out from under his bunk and opened it up. He folded the letter and placed it on top of the stack of letters and latest photographs of seven-year-old Casey, with blonde spit curls. He took out a small brown paper bag from which he pulled a squashed and bedraggled stuffed rabbit and held it up.

"What in hell is that?" Baby-O asked.

"So I shouldn't see my little girl on her birthday empty-handed."

"A fuckin' scratch-ass pink bunny!"

"You got a beef?"

"Noooo—"

"It's all they had at the canteen. Other'n toothpaste and packs of Pall Malls."

"Well now, that's some kind of moldy present, all right."

"I'll remember that on your birthday."

"Shit, you won't even remember my birthday."

"Hell I won't."

Baby-O hugged himself and rocked back and forth on the cot. "Man, I'm gettin' that clammy feel. Bro's better be givin' me my shot before we get on any old aeroplane."

"You feeling poorly?"

"It creeps up, the diabetes. You gotta hand it to a disease that don't never go away, no matter what. Can I see that other thing one more time before you pack it up?"

"Maybe."

"Come on, boss, be kind to me. I got more time ahead, you know."

"Your hands clean?"

"Fuck all, whitey. Gimme it."

Poe took the folded paper out of his breast pocket and handed it to Baby-O, who carefully spread it out on his knees.

"Okay, bro, this time I do it out loud, for real. 'Know all men by these presents: It having been made to appear to the United States Parole Commission that Cameron Poe, inmate number 45936, is eligible to be paroled'—damn! It's all too good to be true."

"Yeah." Cameron looked over at Baby-O, who was staring at the floor. "You'll get your date pretty soon, Baby-O. And when you do, you'll come over to our place for some barbecue."

"For real?"

"Lighten up, for chrissake."

"You think they still have barbecues? Maybe they do everything in them there microwaves now."

"We'll do ribs, steaks, dogs, burgers, chicken."

"Man," Baby-O rocked back, hugging himself, "I can't stop thinking about it."

"We been through some shit, man," Cameron said, replacing the bunny in the banker's box, squashing it down, closing the lid. "We spent some *time*."

Baby-O was changing his shirt, pulling off the one stained with his current sweats. A cockroach scurried for the shadow of the bunk, and Baby-O swatted at it with the damp shirt, the ropelike burn scar on his arm wriggling like a snake.

Cameron Poe shook his head, looking at the scar. "Oh man, what we been through. And if it wasn't for you, in that fire—"

"Now, don't be gettin' all weepy on me, boss." Baby-O pulled on a dry shirt, blue denim prison issue. "We all do what we gotta do. We both coulda been kilt back there. You go out and taste some a that good life, that'll be thanks for me. Long as I get some of that barbecue in time to come. Anyway, we gonna fly a piece together, only difference is I get back in stir after the transfer, you breathe fresh air."

Two guards arrived, and the one with a ring of huge keys opened the cell door. "Okay, Poe, freedom plane's running. Baby-O, let's go."

"I'm going home," Poe said to Baby-O.

"That's a fact."

"Eight years, bro."

"You'll get used to it, bro." In the corridor, Baby-O fell in beside him, behind one guard, in front of the other. "Do me a favor. When you go to a restaurant, don't lick your spoon and stick it in your back pocket."

They walked out to head for their escort out of San Quentin, to Oakland Airport, then to travel on together to their transfer point—Cameron Poe to go home, Baby-O Odell to go on to a new prison to finish out his term.

In a barren office at Oakland Airport, Chief Marshal Allen Devers, of the U.S. Marshal Service, was lecturing two dozen marshals and corrections officers who were bored with the rehash while seriously anticipating their mission.

"Gentlemen," Devers said, "the Marshal's Service annually flies more than a hundred thousand prisoners to various places in the country for transfers, legal hearings, medical exams, and other official matters. As you already know, today's flight is a special one. We're populating Louisiana's Feltham Penitentiary, the newest supermax facility in the institutional system. Feltham is designed to warehouse the worst of the worst. These men are lifers,

...death row. Pure predators, each and every
them. . . ."

Inside the minimum-security blue bus that rolled
through the streets of Oakland, escorted by a single
police cruiser, the men assembled, despite the fact
that they were in handcuffs, waist-chains, and leg
irons, were not the worst of the worst to which
Marshal Devers referred. These ten men were
short-term prisoners, including Cameron Poe, who
was headed to be mustered out, and Baby-O, who
was headed for a minimum-security prison to serve
out his final eighteen months.

"Hey, lady," Baby-O called to the guard walking
slowly up the aisle.

"Lady was a dog in a Walt Disney movie," said
Bishop casually, ambling over and putting a hand
on the seat back. "My name is Bishop. Guard
Bishop to you. Now what do you want?"

"I gotta get my shot before I get on that plane,
Guard Bishop. I missed it last night, and I'm a two-
shot man."

"I'm aware, we're aware," Bishop said. "Your insulin's on board. We'll give it to you after takeoff."

"Yeah, but I don't know these people."

"I'll see to it personally," she said. "Relax. You
ain't goin' nowhere without me."

She consulted her clipboard. "Cameron Poe?"

"Ma'am," Poe said softly.

She turned to him. "You know you're still under federal charge until Carson City, Nevada—that's our transfer point. It's full restraints until you are processed and released, understood?"

"Yes, ma'am, they told me all that."

"Well, just so you're clear on it."

"Just so's I make it home in time for my daughter's birthday."

"I heard you got a daughter."

"I got locked down three months before she was born. She ain't never seen me."

"She didn't visit?"

"I told my wife, no way she was gonna see her daddy in prison, you know, with cons and all that."

"Well, you made a choice. Now at least you got a walking, talking reason to make it go right."

"That I do. Wife, too, you know."

"Goes without saying, doesn't it?"

"I don't think that ever goes without saying."

"You got a point, Poe. Good point."

They arrived on the tarmac just as a twin-engine C-123 Provider cargo plane, white with blue trim and a U.S. Marshals' logo on the nose, was wheeled out of a hangar.

"Welcome to the federal transport system," Guard Bishop said. "Stay put. We gotta sit here a few minutes."

What they were waiting for was the arrival of another bus, this one quite different from the one Cameron Poe arrived in. This one was maximum security: Special armored plates surrounded the blue vehicle; the escort for this was not a single police cruiser but a phalanx of cruisers and motorcycles, lights flashing. This bus held the prisoners to whom Marshal Devers was referring in his address to the guards and marshals who would accompany them on the plane.

This second bus was now approaching the tarmac.

Marshal Vince Larkin hurried down the corridor, boyishly self-conscious about how his new Birkenstocks were squeaking on the tiles. He slid into the back of the room as Chief Marshal Devers was finishing his pep talk.

". . . In the ten years we've been operating, we've never had a breach of security. You men are why." He gave a pause while he looked them over. "It's a point of pride. So today let's exemplify our three operative words: firm, fair, vigilant."

Chief Devers was not a pompous man, nor was he given to making dramatic pronouncements. But he felt obliged to lay down the principles in a diligent, unadorned way before the mission. Then they could all just get down to work.

"Okay," he concluded, "let's get the job done."

The audience milled out. Larkin approached Devers.

"We're down to six offloading in Carson City, chief. All the rest are sheeted to Feltham."

"That's a hellhole from day one, that place."

"Well, it's modern, won't be an Alcatraz."

"You don't know what's going in there. Come on. Let's deal with the DEA boys."

Larkin trailed behind Devers as they hurried down the corridor. He popped his head into an office. "Ginny?"

"Here they are, Vince." Ginny Clark handed him a stack of files. She was, at twenty-five, a new marshal, but with her short blonde hair she looked no more than twenty. "That's all of them. You ready?"

"I'm ready."

"Nope." She walked over and tugged at his tie, to center it. "Now you're ready."

Devers called from the outside doorway, "Let's go, Vince!"

He ran out.

"You're welcome, Vince," Ginny mumbled wistfully to herself as she watched him go. "No problem. Dinner tonight? Sure. . . ."

Larkin and Devers started down the steps when a Corvette convertible wheeled in, squealing to a stop—a fully restored 1964, with a vanity plate reading "AZZ KIKR."

Chief Devers winced. "You know this guy, Vince? Duncan Malloy, DEA. He's as creepy as guys get in our business, if I can be blunt."

Behind the wheel, Malloy, wearing racing gloves and black wraparound sunglasses, stretched. At forty-two, he had been an agent with the U.S. Drug Enforcement Administration for ten years, a Chicago homicide detective before that.

"Duncan!" Devers called, going down the steps. "Good to see you! Beautiful car!"

"Beautiful?" Malloy sat with arms folded across his chest. "Sunsets and Dallas cheerleaders are beautiful, Devers. This buggy is spectacular."

"Like you to meet Vince Larkin, our guy overseeing the transport. Vince? Duncan Malloy, DEA."

"Good to meet you," Larkin said, extending his hand.

Malloy adjusted his sunglasses, ignoring the hand. "Cheers," he said. "I'm sure you know the job."

The maximum-security convoy moved through the airport gates and past the hangars until it reached an area on the outermost tarmac patrolled by Department of Corrections guards in blue jumpsuits and carrying pump shotguns at the ready. At the same time, the C-123 taxied slowly into the area, its rear loading ramp lowering as it came.

From a van, the guards unloaded prisoners' metal banker's boxes, holding their few personal effects, and stowed them in the C-123's tail. Two guards took shotguns from the van and installed them in a rack inside the plane's belly.

The convoy circled the plane and stopped. Guards formed two rows leading from the door of the armored bus. The bus door wheezed open, and prisoners in orange coveralls, hands and feet heavily shackled, started climbing clumsily down the steps, dragging their chains.

Devers, Larkin, Malloy, and a fourth man, DEA Agent William Sims, sat in a surveillance van, watching the scene unfold on a closed-circuit television monitor.

Larkin handed Sims a photo. "This is your man—Francisco Cindino."

Sims studied the eight-by-ten glossy of a dark-haired, handsome, unsmiling man with lean features.

"Son of Eduardo Cindino, the prime mover of narcotics through South America. He's twenty-six. Capable, close-mouthed, hard to track."

"He's a prick," Malloy interrupted, leaning forward to tap his finger on the photo. "Locals busted him running a small courier operation through a small airfield in western Montana. The kid's a potential fountain of information about the family business, but he thinks he's a tough guy. Look at that prick. Like a nice college boy, right? We interrogated him for eight weeks and we got zip."

"We think there's a chance that—" Larkin began.

"This is our last chance before the FBI gets him," Malloy said. "Over my dead body are those assholes getting the credit."

"Okay, okay," Larkin said calmly. "We're picking Cindino up in Carson City. From there to Louisiana you've got two hours of flight time to get him to talk. We got you a seat right next to him. Nobody but us knows who you are. So you're a con. You can ask questions we can't. Cindino is known to be somewhat garrulous in the company of thieves."

"Garrulous?" Malloy planted his fists on his thighs. "What the fuck is garrulous?"

"Talkative, to you, chatty."

Malloy turned to Devers. "What's with this fuckin' dictionary boy here?"

"Maybe you mean thesaurus," Larkin said, with a slight smile.

"Vince," Devers held up his hand, "Malloy, let's take it easy. We got work to do."

"Yeah," Malloy said. He turned to Sims. "You got your weapon, Willie?"

Sims pulled up his right pants leg, exposing a small automatic in an ankle holster.

"Whoa, whoa!" Devers stood up. "Wait a minute here. Nobody's gonna be armed in there."

Larkin nodded. "We've got rules, gentlemen."

"So do we," Malloy said. "Our agents go armed. DEA policy is—"

"All right," Devers said, "let's get this jurisdictional thing out on the table and dealt with right now. This is a U.S. Marshal plane and we are in charge of it."

"No one carries on these flights, guys," Larkin chimed in. "I got a small arsenal of shotguns installed in the belly rack and a .38 in the cockpit lockbox. That's standard. Other than that, we run the plane like a prison—no weapons allowed inside, where inmates could get at them, unless and until there's a call for them. So no weapons in the main cabin of this aircraft, period."

"This is bullshit. My man is not getting on that plane without his gun, period."

"Then your man is not getting on that plane," Larkin said, glancing at Devers who was nodding approval.

Malloy glared at them both. He bared his teeth. He looked at Sims, then looked away. "Okay. Give it to them, Willie. They're holding the cards right this minute."

"Not a good idea," were the first words Sims said since entering the van. He shook his head slowly as he peeled the Velcro loose and handed the holster and gun to Larkin.

"You'll get a receipt," Larkin said.

"Fuck a receipt," Malloy said.

"Your man been briefed on prison behavioral traits?" Devers asked Malloy.

"Jesus, if you guys didn't go by the book you wouldn't go anywhere at all," Malloy said.

"You think I need to know more than I do?" Sims said, raising his eyebrows.

"Doesn't hurt you to hear it," Larkin said. "Ten, twenty years behind bars changes a man, heightens his instincts."

"So does ten, twenty years facing down bad guys," Malloy said.

"Come on, Duncan," Devers said with a sigh. "Give it a rest."

"Avoid eye contact," Larkin continued. "In the joint it's considered an invasion of private space, a sign of aggression, a threat. People get stabbed over somebody locking eyes with them. Make that mistake, it'll give you away in a second."

"I've been around the block a time or two, Larkin."

"Just a reminder. I'm not trying to tell you how

to operate. Just that here you don't have much time, it's a strange situation."

"I'll handle it. Jesus, what's *that*?"

Their eyes fastened on the monitor, which showed a green military Huey helicopter dropping low over the C-123, and in its open side door sat two men with shotguns trained toward the ground.

"I told you," Devers said quietly, "this load is special."

The first prisoner appeared on the monitor, a slight, blond man shuffling in leg irons. On his wrist was a plastic bracelet, and a guard scanned it with an electronic gun to read the bar code before allowing the man to shuffle on up the ramp into the plane.

"That's William Bedford," Larkin read from a file. "Aka Billy Bedlam."

"The mass murderer?"

"The same. Came home one night after a church fellowship meeting, found his wife in bed with his cousin. Left them alone and drove four towns over to his wife's family's house. Killed her parents and her brothers and sisters with her father's .45 from World War II. Even her dog. Told the cops his only regret was that his wife didn't have more parents and brothers and sisters, because he had more bullets."

They watched Billy Bedlam disappear into the plane.

"This next guy, the black guy with the shaved head, that's Nathan Jones, aka 'Diamond Dog.' Former general of the Black Guerrillas that terrorized Toledo."

"What's that on his neck?" Malloy asked.

"That's a tattoo of the continent of Africa. Got his name because, if you'll look close and he happens to smile, he's got a diamond shaped like a star embedded in a front tooth. His hands are ducttaped to keep him from grabbing anything. He blew up a meeting of the National Rifle Association in 1988. Said they represented the 'basest negativity of the white race.' "

"That's a quote?"

"That's a quote. Another one is that he used to brag that he'd 'killed more men than cancer.' "

They watched the guards frisk Diamond Dog.

"He's a literate guy. Wrote a book in prison: *Reflections in a Diamond Eye*, which got good reviews for its assessment of the black community. There's still talk it may be a movie one day. But this guy'd likely blow up the theaters if he got loose. He sure knows how."

The solemn parade continued, prisoner by prisoner shuffling toward the open ramp of the plane in their leg irons connected to their waists by chains, and wrist irons; the guards frisked them, scanned their bracelet bar codes, and led them aboard.

"The guy with the shaved head and the goofy smile is Cyrus Grissom, aka 'Cyrus the Virus.'"

"Oh, for chrissake!" Malloy shook his head. "Who the hell gives them these names?"

"They earn 'em," Larkin said, "just like on the outside. Only difference is, it's not for the public or the cops, it's for their own in-group. Lot of tongue-in-cheek. But this bozo's done it all—kidnapping, murder, robbery, extortion. Thirty-nine years old, twenty-five of them in institutions. And he's got serious juice inside the system."

"Meaning?"

"Got big-time respect, a leader. Inside he's earned two degrees, engineering and psychology. Killed three inmates, suspected in eight more deaths. Incited three riots. Escaped twice."

"Escaped *twice*? What the hell kind of institutions they running out there?"

"Bribed guards once, substituted a look-alike who had AIDS another time. Very clever guy. I'd say he's a true product of the system."

"What kind of bullshit is that? You one of those sociologists thinks we're responsible for breeding these assholes?"

"No, just that this guy learned the system inside and out and used it."

"They should just fly the fucking plane into the side of a mountain, do mankind a favor."

Devers chuckled. "Don't think that hasn't been discussed. Agent Sims, you're gonna be surrounded by an interesting society while you try to pump that Cindino guy."

"Don't worry about it," Sims said.

FOUR

Guard Chick Falzon, a hulking veteran, frisked Billy Bedlam harshly, patting him down with callused hands.

"Move me, baby," Billy giggled.

When the next prisoner approached, Falzon said, feigning awe, "Diamond Dog Jones, well my, my, my. This bunch is like the scumbag all-star team."

"You might say we're all good at what we do," Jones said, "speaking scumbag to scumbag, that is. You don't miss your water till your well runs dry, my friend."

"Hidden meanings turn me on, pal."

"Well, think about it."

He was led away, replaced by Cyrus Grissom.

"The Virus," Falzon acknowledged.

"Hello. And hooray for air travel."

"What you got up your sleeve this time, Virus?" Falzon said, patting him down.

Cyrus the Virus just smiled before clanking away in his irons to board the plane.

It wasn't until the maximum-security prisoners had been safely loaded that the bus bearing Cameron Poe and Baby-O pulled into the loading zone. They unloaded the same way the other bus had and went through the same procedures.

Eventually, Poe stood to be frisked. Guard Falzon felt around his breast pocket, stuck his fingers in, and pulled out the latest snapshot of Casey.

"No personal items," Falzon said.

"It's my daughter," Poe said.

"I don't care if it's the weeping momma of Christ," Falzon said, slipping the photo into his own shirt pocket. "You know the rules."

"I'm getting out," Poe said.

Falzon stepped up and put his face right in front of Poe's, an inch away. "You ain't out yet, boy. I am *God* to you for this flight. You can have a good ride or you can have a bad ride."

Poe felt Falzon's spit on his cheek.

Guard Bishop walked by, checking numbers off on her clipboard. "Easy, boys," she said. "There's enough root beer for everybody. Move along, Poe."

· · ·

In the surveillance van, Malloy watched the mute debate. "Who's that?"

Larkin flipped through pages in his file, coming to the photo of the man with Falzon. "Cameron Poe. He's nobody. Let's go."

"I can't emphasize too much, Agent Sims," Devers said, "that no one on the flight knows your classification, not even my guards. I know you've done deep undercover on the ground, but this is in the air. No one can reach you, if it goes wrong. So keep your wheels on the ground."

"Let's just do it," Sims said.

The group exited the van. Sims walked stiffly ahead of Larkin, as if in custody.

Malloy and Devers followed a few paces behind. "Tell me, chief," Malloy said, "is the U.S. Marshal Service in the habit of employing annoying wiseass bookworm creeps?"

"Larkin's one of our best, Duncan. Be a good idea for you to believe that."

"Yeah, well I'd still like to crush his larynx with my boot."

"Charming thought, Malloy, but not altogether professional—wouldn't you say?"

Larkin walked behind Sims down the phalanx of guards with shotguns. "Have a good flight," he said to them.

"Thanks, Vince . . . Right . . . You got it, boss."

He came to Guard Bishop. "How's the golf game?"

"Just like everything else, the balls are too small."

Larkin chuckled. "Enjoy the flight."

"See you later, Vince."

Sims had his bar code read, and Falzon approached to frisk him.

Malloy stepped up and flashed his badge. "I got him."

Falzon nodded and backed off.

Malloy patted Sims's shirt down, then squatted and slid his hands down his pants legs. The right leg, which had held the revolver Sims was forced to give up, was smooth. The left leg had an almost indiscernible lump. Malloy looked up at Sims and gave an almost indiscernible wink.

Cameron Poe stepped off the ramp into the main cabin to be confronted with the grim scene of how the plane was configured for the transport of dangerous passengers. The cabin was divided roughly into three parts that could be separated by doors of thick wire mesh, which were now open. Two rows of seats flanked the aisle to the rear. Up ahead there was a row of four single-man cages of wire mesh and black steel bars, their doors open. Occupying the front three were Cyrus "the Virus" Grissom, Nathan "Diamond Dog" Jones, and William "Billy Bedlam" Bedford. The fourth cage was empty.

Falzon strode through the cabin to a control board and hit a button. Lights above the cages went from green to red, and the doors clanged shut. Poe took a seat at the rear, two seats behind Baby-O, as Falzon came back up the aisle, making entries on a checklist. He stuck his big marker pen in his breast pocket. Agent Bishop instantly reached over to grab the pen.

"Uh, everything's a weapon, right?"

"Oh, right, shit. Wasn't thinking." Falzon took the pen back and clipped it to a chain around his neck and dropped it under his shirt.

"Hey, friend."

Poe turned to the man seated across the aisle, a black con with a weasel face and a sly smile.

"I'm Pinball Parker. Armed robber, arsonist, dope fiend." He smiled like a ferret. "Hell of a nice guy."

Poe nodded to him without speaking.

Pinball turned to the man seated immediately beside him, a man with straight black hair in a ponytail, a fine, prominent nose, dark skin. "So you're a native, huh? What's up, Cochise? What tribe you hail from?"

The man stared straight ahead.

"Okay, okay," Pinball said, "don't go gettin' all Wounded Knee on me. We'll hunt beaver together a couple moons from now. Haw!"

A guard led Agent Sims onto the plane, directed him to a preassigned seat directly behind Poe. Poe noticed Billy Bedlam watching Sims from his cage.

Bedlam noticed Poe watching him. "You eyeballin' me, punk?" he growled at Poe.

"I was just admiring your place," Poe said. "Looks comfortable."

"Admire *this*," Bedlam said, grabbing his crotch.

Poe looked away.

Ahead of him, Baby-O was leaning forward in his seat, calling to the white-jacketed medic sorting his gear at the front of the cabin.

"Hey, Doc, I need my shot!"

The medic walked back. "My name is Chambers. You'll get your shot when we're airborne."

"Aw, what's the difference? Why not now?"

Chambers turned and walked away. Baby-O knew how it worked: Nobody in the prison system has to answer anybody about anything.

"These fuckers won't be happy 'til I go into a deep, dark, tropical coma," Baby-O muttered.

Chief in-flight guard Chick Falzon, having attended to checklists and paperwork, now strode the aisle intoning his message to the assembled inmates.

"Well, well, well! Here we are, all together, cozy as bugs in a rug—I can vouch for the bugs. We got out-and-out celebrities in here. I mean, take a look at yourselves! We got people who wrote books, people who been on television, people talked about all over the place. But I gotta tell you, I ain't impressed."

Falzon turned and strode back the other way. "So let's get this straight, gentlemen, or bugs. We got rules, we up here in Con Air. Number one: Keep your hands in your laps. I know you like 'em there anyway. Number two: Keep the noise down. That means you will not yell, scream, or holler, you will speak seldom and quietly. Number three: If you spit, if you bite, if you stomp your feet, if you look a way I don't like, you will get our own special treatment. . . ."

"Fuck you, pig!" came a voice from behind Falzon. As he turned around, he caught a wad of spit on his cheek. He strode toward the offender, a young man with a shaved head and a swastika tattooed on his hand.

"Gag and bag this Nazi muffin," Falzon ordered, pointing him out.

Three other guards surrounded the man quickly,

slapped wide gray duct tape over his mouth, a nylon mesh stocking over his head.

"These rules will be enforced," Falzon continued, unfazed. "If not, I *will be* gargling testicles. Understood?" He looked around, meeting the gazes of the assembled cons, none of whom nodded or made any sign at all.

Cyrus the Virus looked out of his cage, holding onto the bars and pressing his face against them. "Hey, you," he called to a man whose forearms bore tattoos of Chicano pachuco gangs. The man looked around. "Are you a notorious criminal, friend?"

"Fuck yeah," the man said. "You don't know me? They call me 'Johnny Twenty-Three.'"

"You're Johnny Twenty-Three? My oh my, of course I know of you. You're clubbed in with the Tex-Mex Mafia. Am I right? Serving seven life sentences for rape, twenty-three counts of rape. Am I right?"

Johnny pushed up his rolled-up sleeve even further to reveal twenty-three tiny tattoos of red hearts. He puffed out his chest with pride. "One of dese for each of my twenty-three lucky ladies." He paused to leer at Guard Bishop as she walked by, ignoring the banter. Then he grinned. "If they knew the truth, I'd be called 'Johnny Six Hundred.'"

Cyrus frowned. "Actually, I do despise rapists,

more than just about anybody or thing. Somewhere between cockroaches and spittle. So, generally I would gladly string up such a person as you by the balls, which I would paint with honey to attract bees. I hope you understand." He suddenly grinned. "But with you, I'll make an exception, for the time being, at least."

Johnny seemed bemused. He turned away.

"Falzon," Cyrus called to the guard who was walking by. "What's the in-flight movie today?"

"It's a good one, Cyrus. Called *I'll Never Make Love to a Woman on the Beach Again.*"

"You're a funny fellow."

"And it's preceded by the award-winning short: *No More Steak for Me Ever.*"

"Precious."

The rear ramp was raised and sealed, the white-and-blue Provider taxied to the runway with its odd cargo: all manacled, four in cages, one so far with a mouth taped and a head covered by nylon mesh.

From the window in the marshals' office, Larkin stood and watched the plane take off and begin a slow upward bank to the left.

Ginny Clark came up behind him, smoothing the sides of her skirt as if she were about to walk on stage. "I hope all this goes okay," she said softly.

"Of course it will, why not?" he said without turning. "Just another transport flight, some transfers, some hard cases. Nothing we haven't handled before, more or less. After all, this is a well-oiled machine." Now he turned to give her a brief smile.

"I'm sorry," she said. "I'm just a kook sometimes."

"No you're not." He touched her shoulder lightly, causing in her the slightest shiver. "You're just conscientious."

"That's me," she mumbled, as he turned back to the window to watch the twin dark exhausts from the C-123 spread into the ether. "The runner-up from South Dakota, Miss Conscientious."

"By the way, did you return that phone call from Washington?"

"Yup. Your expense check is in the mail."

"Thanks, babe. I gotta finish up that paperwork." He brushed by her on the way out.

"Babe," she muttered, as her shoulders sagged. "*Babe?*"

The plane leveled off, and as soon as he was sure of the equilibrium of steady flight, Cyrus the Virus hunched over on the seat in his steel cage and with his fingernail began to pick idly at a callus on the heel of his hand. He glanced up to see Guard Falzon pause at the cage of Diamond Dog.

Falzon leaned close to the cage. "What's the good word these days, Doggie Do?" He smiled at Diamond Dog's icy glare. "Don't tell me! You found Allah in the joint! That's it, ain't it? If you wanna bow down and face the east, it's a little to your left."

"We're all yoked to the same chariot, my friend," Diamond Dog said, calmly, unblinking.

"That a fact? Well, then how come I'm walking around loose out here?" Falzon walked away chortling.

Bishop was patrolling the area of seats toward the rear. "How you doing, Poe?"

"Fine. You got a first name, Guard Bishop?"

"No, it's just Bishop. Like Prince. Or Cher. You know, Madonna . . ."

"It works for you . . ."

"It's Sally . . ."

"Sally Bishop. Sounds like an astronaut. Or a schoolteacher."

"There's a little bit of both in this gig, lemme tell ya."

In the cage next to Cyrus's, Diamond Dog was similarly picking at a callus on the heel of his hand. Both kept an eye on the guards walking to and fro.

Cyrus looked toward the rear of the plane and nodded slightly.

Poe noticed Pinball, across the aisle, seem to ac-
knowledge the nod. Pinball glanced around, keeping tabs on the guards. In those odd moments
when they had moved away from the immediate
area, Pinball would stick his fingers into his mouth
and appear to be picking at his teeth.

Then Poe noticed that bit by bit Pinball was
pulling a slender thread—dental floss—out of his
mouth. He thought it odd, to be flossing on this
flight. Then the thread became longer, became a
foot long, longer still, hidden in his hand.

Poe watched this, puzzled, without turning his
head toward Pinball. The Indian beside Pinball
kept staring straight ahead. Pinball kept surrepti-
tiously pulling out the ever-lengthening tiny string
of floss from his mouth.

Suddenly the string ended. A tiny blob of wax
on the end of the string dropped into his hand.
Pinball closed his hand and looked casually around.

The string, Poe assumed, had been swallowed
some time ago by Pinball, and the tiny ball of wax
at the end of it had been resting in his stomach ever
since.

Using his thumb and forefinger, Pinball subtly
broke the wax apart, and for an instant Poe caught
a glimpse of a clear tube and the blue tip of the end
of a match.

In the cage further forward, unseen by Poe, Cyrus continued picking at the callus on the heel of his hand until finally the tip of a slightly flattened pin emerged. He palmed the pin, worked it into position between his hidden fingers, and, appearing simply to cross his wrists, inserted the pin into the lock and began working it back and forth to spring the mechanism.

In the adjacent cage, Diamond Dog went through the same maneuver. Both men worked to open their handcuffs.

Baby-O was oblivious to anything else going on in the cabin except what the medic, Chambers, was doing. Finally Chambers got to him, carrying a syringe and a plastic packet of ampules of insulin.

"About time," Baby-O said with a sigh.

"Okay, left arm," Chambers said.

"You can have my left arm, right arm, and both feet," Baby-O said, turning his left arm palm up.

Chambers pushed the blue sleeve up a little further, swabbed the arm, and gave him the shot.

Pinball, meanwhile, turned slowly to Poe and winked. Then he turned slowly back toward the Indian. "Hey, Cochise," he whispered, at the same time that he squirted liquid from the tiny tube onto the Indian's seat. Almost in the same motion, he flicked his thumbnail across the blue-tipped match, sparking it, and tossed it onto the Indian's seat.

Flames burst up around the Indian, who screamed and tried to rise.

Pinball leaped up and screamed at the same time: "Fire! Fire! He's a fucking witch doctor!"

Guards raced down the aisle with fire extinguishers and began spraying the seat.

"He did spontaneous combustion!" Pinball yelled, extending a shaking finger at the collapsed Indian. "This man is a witch doctor! He just went on fire, the fucking bastard! I ain't sittin' next to no crazy witch doctor!"

While the guards were occupied with the frantic action of putting out the fire, Pinball was slowly backing away, up the aisle, toward the cages. "Put him out! Put him out!" he hollered. He edged back. He came even with the controls. With a quick, darting move, he reached out to the cage levers, flipped up the safety catch, and yanked down the first of the four in the row. The cage light switched from red to green.

A Klaxon alarm blared through the plane at the same time that Diamond Dog's cage door slid open. Guard Bishop lunged for Pinball. Diamond Dog charged out of his cage, grabbing the first man in front of him, who was the medic Chambers, throwing his arm around his neck and lifting him and burying the hasp of one of his handcuffs into

Chambers' throat. Chambers emitted a gurgle, flailing with his legs and wildly grabbing for the lethal cuff stuck in his neck. Diamond Dog whirled him around, and his flailing legs hit an onrushing guard in the face. The guard staggered backward into the wall, and Chambers' kicking feet hit the button that released the rear hatch.

The ramp began to lower, wind whipped through the cabin. Guards converged on Diamond Dog, swarming him, driving him down, while he bucked and kicked. The ampules scattered from Chambers' plastic pouch, and in the melee, feet trampled them.

"Get the fuck off my insulin!" Baby-O screeched, squirming in his restraints.

Guard Falzon grabbed a taser gun from a cabinet in the galley and fired two jolts of electricity into Diamond Dog, sending him into a writhing collapse on the floor.

Pinball wrestled with Bishop and managed to struggle free for a moment to throw the second lever, opening the cage of Cyrus the Virus. The Virus shot out from the cage, slamming into the nearest guard with his forearm, dropping him cold. He raced for the cockpit, where a guard braced himself. Cyrus swung his cuffs, raking the guard's face, sending him stumbling to the side.

At the sight of Cyrus, the copilot reached into the lockbox under his seat and pulled out the only real gun on board, the .38, and fired wildly twice in the direction of the con. Cyrus dove aside. The bullets dropped two cons in the main cabin, one through the head, the other through the chest. Cyrus bloodied the copilot's face with his cuffs, blinding him. The pilot yanked back on the yoke, jerking the plane's nose up.

The copilot sagged against the instrument panel. Cyrus dropped to his knees to grab the gun and fired a shot into the man's forehead. The pilot was reaching for the emergency button under the dials.

Cyrus put the gun to his head. "Say there was a brief disturbance, but everything's under control. Or I'll kill you."

"No, you won't," the pilot said stoically. "Without me, there's no one to fly the plane."

"Oh yes, I will." He clicked back the hammer. "I don't think that far ahead."

The pilot picked up the mike. "Uh, Carson City? Scratch that alarm. We had a little dustup, but everything's okay now . . ."

Cyrus slid out of the cabin, where the melee between cons and guards continued. Bishop had Pinball's face against the wall, trying to establish a hammerlock on him. Falzon, with a long cut on his cheek dripping blood, was taking a series of left hooks from Diamond Dog.

Cyrus fired off two quick shots in the direction of the blaring Klaxon, stilling it, freezing the action.

"Listen up, everybody!" he bellowed into the suddenly silenced cabin, as eyes fastened on him. "This is your captain speaking! Welcome to Con Air!"

A cheer went up, along with several manacled pairs of fists.

"Falzon!" He pointed to the guard with the bleeding face. "The keys, if you please!" He held up his own unlocked cuffs. "The keys for these!"

The cons roared approval and held up their handcuffed wrists.

Cameron Poe sat riveted in his seat—through all this he had not stood. He was so close to freedom; all this was the worst turn of events in the world. Baby-O turned around to look at him, his own eyes showing dismay over the more immediate disaster facing him—that he had to have insulin soon or risk going into diabetic shock. They were the only two among the cons who weren't cheering this uprising.

A silent alarm button flashed red on the console, while ordinary radio communications crackled between tower and planes at the Oakland Airport air-traffic control center.

"Roger that, Carson City," Ginny Clark said into the mike. "Clark out." She sat back with a sigh of relief just as Vince Larkin burst into the room.

"What the hell happened?" he asked breathlessly.

"Calm down, Vince. Just a sort of false alarm. They had a little ruckus up there, and the pilot reacted too fast and hit the emergency alarm. But then when he found out what was really going on, he checked in to say everything's fine."

. "What the hell's a little ruckus?"

"Maybe somebody just started hollering or getting belligerent or something. This pilot's never flown this number before."

"What kind of crap is that? You don't hit the emergency button just because you hear a noise. Get that guy on the horn."

"Take it easy, Vince. You don't want to embarrass the guy in front of the crew by questioning his judgment while he's flying up there. Everything's cool. See? The alarm's not flashing. The transponder is confirming location and direction. Everything's okay. It's not like you to get worked up."

"Yeah, Ginny, you're right. I don't know why I'm jumpy. We've never had quite this mix before."

"That's not the problem, though, the cons, right?"

He thought for a moment. "No, you're right. The mix includes the ringer, Sims. Not just him being aboard as an undercover agent looking for information, but because of their attitude. They wanted guns on board, for chrissake. They probably think guards should carry guns in prisons, too, like an invitation to some crazy inmates to jump them and take their weapons and cause a real ruckus."

"These guys aren't typical DEA."

"Well, yes and no. My experience is that those guys tend to get a little hot-eyed. But to get confrontational about carrying a gun on this type of aircraft, to want to override our rules, that's not necessarily typical, no. Anyway, I guess that's what's making me jumpy. They can't finish that flight fast enough for me."

Ginny smiled at him. "Well, meanwhile, here we are, sort of stuck on duty, until we finish this thing. Might as well make the best of it, huh? Want to order in a Japanese lunch? I'll serve you like a geisha."

"No, thanks." He stared off, distracted.

He wasn't even listening, she thought. She chuckled.

"Something funny?" he said, not unkindly, abruptly returning his attention to her.

"No. Just thinking about, uh, that airplane up there."

"Her cargo's ugly. But her constitution is strong."

"Yup. Her constitution is tough as Kevlar, Vince." She smiled at him.

FIVE

The back hatch finally hissed shut, and the rush of backdraft abated throughout the cabin. Papers and bits of stuff, things that had blown loose here and there—instructions, files, eucalyptus leaves, plastic sheets, rags—settled to the floor. The Provider cruised with deceptive smoothness at 15,000 feet.

Cameron Poe silently assessed the details of everything he saw. His mission, which had seemed so straightforward and inexorable an hour earlier, was just to get home safely. But now that mission was threatened from a dozen different directions. A planeload of hard-time cons contained instability per se—the instability of two halves of a critical mass in proximity but not explosive unless rammed together. The cons had been manacled, four of the riskiest had been caged, half a dozen guards patrolled them all. It was, it should have been, a simple transfer, no riskier than moving them in a prison from one wing to another.

But the desperation of long-termers whose minds were honed to eerie capabilities by the very nature of their lives required constant vigilance under the best of conditions. The best of conditions were in a maximum-security prison. A Provider cargo plane could never provide the best of conditions. What was assumed was that it would work because security was careful and tight, and the flight was short. Now, however, some of these honed brains had conspired to break the security.

But how far could this breach go, isolated as they all were aloft in an aircraft with finite range? These cons, or at least some of them, would easily risk death. Death for everybody including Cameron Poe. But first they would try to get free. For that, they would need to get back to the earth somewhere.

Cameron's mission—indeed, his duty—had now become to dope out what the next steps would be, what his next steps should be. He had to be keenly watchful, of course. But he would also have to take steps along the way. Those steps would be determined by his meticulous assessment of the situation: what steps others were taking, what personalities were in control, what the relationships were, what they could get away with, what he could get away with. Mistakes here, as in a commando action, would likely be fatal. But of course here, as in a commando action, you might die anyway, without making any false moves at all.

The guards were arrayed against the bulkhead separating the cabin from the cockpit. Cyrus the Virus, pacing back and forth in front of them, stopped before Guard Bishop.

"I need a traffic report," he said to her, his face close to hers. "I need the numbers for Carson City."

"Numbers?"

"You know, how many on, how many off?"

"I wouldn't know."

He reached out to caress her neck. She flinched.

"She really doesn't know," Guard Falzon piped up. "I've got the manifest here." He pulled the sheets from inside his shirt and looked at them. "Shows six off, ten on, and—"

Cyrus snatched the manifest from Falzon's hand. "I didn't ask you for a book report."

"I thought you—"

Cyrus grabbed Falzon's lips and squeezed them together, as he smiled. He handed the manifest to Pinball, whose rodentlike features were, in this tense atmosphere, even more pinched. Pinball's nose wiggled as if he were testing the air.

"What you want with this?" Pinball said.

"Find the six. Then crack the rest."

Pinball moved down the aisle, checking name tags against his manifest, unlocking the shackles on some, bypassing others.

"Hey!" shouted one whom he'd skipped, waving his wrists. "Get these things off me! What the fuck you doing?"

"Cork it, pal, you'll figure it out. Otherwise, none of your business."

Baby-O was released, and he quickly squatted in the aisle to pick through the debris for any unbroken insulin ampules he could find.

Cameron Poe forced himself to relax as Pinball bent down to unlock his cuffs and chains. This was not the moment for action. Pinball said nothing to him, didn't make eye contact at all, just opened the locks and moved on.

Pinball eyed Billy Bedlam through the bars of his cage. "I let you out, Billy, you gonna play nice? Huh?"

"Hey, how else would I play? You guys are my heroes. Don't you know that?"

"You'll never know what I know, pal," Pinball said. He nodded to Cyrus who nodded to Diamond Dog, who pulled the lever that changed the light from red to green and opened Bedlam's cage.

Bedlam stepped out and looked around with a shy grin as if he'd tracked mud into a museum.

When the six were freed, they set about, under Cyrus's direction, to chain the guards to the bars and mesh of the cages.

Cameron Poe heard muttering behind him: "This is so fucked up, so fucked up. . . ."

Now he could rise and turn to face the man he didn't know was Agent Sims. Sims was sweating profusely.

"Why the fuck are you freed up while I'm still locked here?" he growled.

"You're sitting next to an empty seat," Poe said. "Maybe that's why."

"What the fuck difference would that make?"

Poe turned away.

Johnny Twenty-Three sidled up to Agent Bishop, rubbing his wrist. He extended his right forearm and pointed to the hearts. "I got a space here, see? Right after the last one. Just for you. Got your name all over it. I'll make a new little heart, that'll be you."

"Well, that's fine news, creep," she said calmly.

Just as he put a hand on her breast, Johnny was spun around and slammed against the mesh next to her.

"I can't allow that," Cameron Poe said, clamping a hand on Johnny's throat and speaking softly.

"You know who I am?" Johnny said, pushing Poe's hand away.

"I know enough."

Johnny started to take a swing, but Poe struck first, knuckles to the diaphragm, and Johnny sank harmlessly to the floor.

Others gathered quickly around. Poe faced them. "Be cool," he said, fanning his palms out. "Nothing's happening, not here, not now."

Cyrus pushed through the group. "He's right. Everybody back off. This is not the time or the place."

They dutifully backed off and dispersed.

Cyrus put his face up to Johnny's and smiled. "Can you fly, Johnny, without this plane?"

"No. What you mean?"

"I mean, be careful how you look at her. Because if your dick goes outta your pants, you go outta this plane. You understand?"

Johnny pouted, then nodded. "But you wouldn't throw me out."

"You wanna bet on that? Huh, Johnny? I want a piece just as bad as you, boy. But more than that I wanna get out of here. If you wanna get out before me, from way up here, you just touch her one time. You'll fly, boy."

Cyrus patted his cheek.

Diamond Dog leaned to Cyrus's ear. "The pilot wants to know what he's supposed to do, because he doesn't have unlimited fuel."

"He'll land at Carson City Airport, just as his schedule calls for."

Dog nodded, but Billy Bedlam danced around.

"Carson City?" he whined. "Where the law is? Where they'll be waitin' for us? You outta your fucking mind?"

"Well," Cyrus faced him, "you might say yes, according to various psychological evaluations of which I've been apprised. Sit down, Bedlam." He looked off down the aisle to check the progress of Pinball, who was unlocking more ankle restraints. "Diamond Dog, if you'll be so kind, you can explain the facts of life to these assembled gentlemen."

The unchained convicts crowded around, puzzled, exchanging glances, giddy with the wild, unexpected action.

Diamond Dog looked up and down the aisle, taking in all the convicts. "Now, boys. You think you're free 'cause your cuffs and chains been cracked. But you're not free, not yet. You're up here in the air. We can't stay up here forever. We got to set down to carry this out. I'm not gonna be repeating this little chat, so listen carefully. Because if you don't, you may be the next to be dead. Now, those other two boys there, that wasn't their fault. But it's a lesson how delicate this can be. The copilot up there, he made a bad move. That cost those other two boys. Any bad move can cost any one of us.

"Now. Down there, at the next stop, Carson City, we're gonna have a bunch of U.S. marshals waiting on us with shotguns. That's substantial. But we can handle it. If you do exactly what we tell you, the rest of our lives will be a vacation in a nonextradition country."

"What's a nontradition country?" interrupted one of the cons.

"Non*extra*dition, you idiot. Means a country that won't throw you out just 'cause the United States asks them to send you back. It means you can *stay* there. We'll have sandy beaches, drinks with little umbrellas in them, dirty naked girls."

"Like a *vacation*!" somebody said.

"Like a *paid* vacation," Diamond Dog said.

"What do you mean, paid vacation?" Billy Bedlam said. "Who's doing the paying?"

Diamond Dog looked at Cyrus the Virus.

"Our employer," Cyrus said, smiling. "Francisco Cindino."

"Who the fuck is that?"

"You'll find out. He's got more money than God. He'll be joining us soon."

"What the fuck . . . Imagine that . . . How's he gonna get on board? . . . I heard of him . . ." The cons looked at each other.

Cameron Poe caught the twitch in the eye of Agent Sims and wondered what it meant. It was something that mattered.

"That's it," Diamond Dog said. "That's all you need to know right now."

The cons started moving around.

Cyrus walked down the aisle to Pinball. "Who's supposed to get off at Carson City?"

"These three," he said, pointing to Poe and two convicts still chained in their seats. "And guys named Dalton, Hernandez and Jackson."

"And where, my friend, are Dalton, Hernandez, and Jackson?"

"I'm on it."

"It's only six cons altogether," Diamond Dog said. "It shouldn't take you a week."

"Hey, it ain't so simple."

Cyrus chuckled, eyeing Pinball. "They've got name tags. You can't read, can you, my defective friend?"

"If I had to, I could read."

Cyrus clapped him on the back. "Go ahead on, Pinball, feel your way through it. You got five minutes."

Pinball scurried away.

Cameron Poe, one of the three cons left of the six originally scheduled to get off, listened to the exchange. From time to time he looked around ca-

sually, always calculating, sizing things up, gauging
the strengths and weak spots, assessing the eyes of
the others, their movements.

That's why he noticed the carefully concealed
movements of the man he wondered about, the
man who had been sweating before his restraints
were removed, the man who was not a con but in
fact William Sims, an agent with the Drug Enforcement Administration. He noticed the man
slowly bending down and reaching toward his
ankle.

Vince Larkin poked his head into Ginny's office.
"I'm starving. Could you stand some Chinese food,
or Japanese?"

"I asked you before," she said, swiveling in her
chair to face him.

"Asked me what?"

"I said I'd serve you like a geisha."

He laughed. "Why don't you go ahead and
order us some stuff? You choose." He walked away,
chuckling to himself. She was cute as a button. He
could be interested in her, but he was sure she
thought of nothing but her job.

Ginny, on the other hand, chuckled too, because
her perception was that he never noticed her, never
would notice her, and she could flirt and suggest

until her face was as blue as her blazer—Vince Larkin was one of those bachelors you could dance naked in front of, and they'd never notice you at all.

She picked up the phone to order Italian. She wondered if he'd notice the difference.

SIX

It was just the quickest glimpse, would have been no more than a small dark shadow to most people, maybe just a scar on the side of the ankle. To Cameron Poe, though, it was a hidden, black .25 automatic. Instantly he knew that, whatever this guy was, he wasn't one of the convicts, and whatever he had in mind, it was trouble.

"Easy, pal," Poe said softly.

With that, Agent Sims snatched the gun from his ankle holster and sprang up, aiming first at Poe, then turning toward the others. "Everybody freeze!" he hollered.

Heads turned, eyes widened.

"Who the fuck are you?" Pinball said, stepping toward him.

Sims grabbed Pinball, spun him around, held him in a choke hold with one arm while he stuck the gun to his ear with the other. "DEA is who the fuck I am!"

"Sorry I asked," Pinball said.

"You don't stand still, you'll be a hell of a lot sorrier!"

Pinball stopped squirming.

Cyrus had his arm extended, at the end of it a .38 directed at Sims.

"Drop it!" Sims commanded.

"I'll be with you in a moment," Cyrus said. He whirled to grab Guard Bishop with a choke hold mimicking the one Sims had on Pinball, and planted the gun in her ear just like Sims' in Pinball's. "Now then, you were saying?"

"I was saying I'm DEA. You know what that means? We got a policy about hostages, which is I don't give a shit about that guard!"

"What it means, DEA man, is that you're most likely as big a crook as anybody else up here." Cyrus began moving up the aisle toward Sims, keeping Bishop in front of him. Cyrus and Sims locked eyes, so did Bishop and Pinball, who apparently would be the sacrifices in a shoot-out.

Cameron Poe edged slightly toward a space between them, weighing the prospects.

"Back off, con," Cyrus said to Poe without looking at him. "This ain't your play."

Poe stayed where he was.

"Now," Cyrus said, clucking. "What the heck is a DEA man doing on this particular airplane flight? I declare, that's odd. Won't they fly you boys commercial? They too cheap to pay for you?"

"Stop right there!" Sims ordered.

"Couldn't you sell enough drugs to take care of yourself, DEA man?" Cyrus stopped a couple of yards away. "Or did you just get yourself so strung out you couldn't book a flight?"

"I'll do your man, right here!"

"Next time you're selecting a human shield," Cyrus said, sighing, "you'd be better off choosing something other than a two-bit Negro crackhead."

"I ain't two-bit," Pinball said.

Bishop shifted her gaze to Sims. "Shoot him. You know the rules. Don't play around with him. Do it!"

"Quiet, sweetheart," Cyrus said, twisting the barrel in her ear.

Poe took a chance, took a step out toward Sims, who was in over his head. "I think you better drop the gun, cowboy. There's no way out, this way."

"Oh yeah?"

"You can't control this."

"Oh no?"

There was a hint of movement behind Sims. He spun and fired, hitting the offending con in the mouth, blowing his face apart. "How's that for control, asshole?"

"Very impressive," Cyrus said, taking the opportunity to move a step closer.

"Easy now," Poe said, looking at Cyrus, then at Sims. "You got a chance, if you give me that gun. You got a chance to live."

Sims now stared fully at Poe. "You crazy bast—"

That was when Cyrus fired the .38, blowing off the section of Sims' head around his ear. Sims fell forward onto Pinball, who tossed him off with disgust.

"That dumb piece of shit prob'ly didn't even have a real job," Pinball said, stooping to recover the gun.

Cyrus flung Bishop away and turned to Poe. Bishop recovered her balance and stood stolidly in front of the cages, revealing nothing with her face.

"Well now, convict," Cyrus said in a friendly tone, holding out his hand to Pinball for the gun, which Pinball reluctantly gave him, "what's your name?"

"Cameron Poe."

"Very nice work, Cameron Poe. You been around the block, I can tell. You and me can work together, maybe. Don't get any other ideas." With that, Cyrus walked back toward the front of the cabin, never once glancing at Sims where he fell.

Poe did look at the body of Agent Sims. The body told him that Sims was most likely what he said—no prison pallor, no calluses, plus the fact that to get in on this situation with a .25 strapped to your ankle you almost had to be an agent for somebody. DEA sounded about right. The gun you could pick up anywhere. The holster was government issue. Those DEA bastards had steel balls, would do almost anything, including run roughshod over rights, deal drugs if they felt like it, play like power-mad cowboys.

"You all right?" Poe asked Guard Bishop, watching the convicts warily crowd around the messy body of Agent Sims.

"I been better. You oughta stay as far outta this as you can, with your status."

Poe slid into the seat next to Baby-O, who was looking a little peaked. "How you feeling, bro?"

Baby-O spread his fingers and waggled his hand. "Hey, nice job, bro. First of all, you didn't save the federal dude's life, while you could just as well been blown out yourself. And second, you give out that you're new best friends with the Virus dude. What's up, my man?"

"Taking it a step at a time, bro."

Up toward the cockpit, Cyrus studied a flight plan. Pinball walked up, shaking his head.

"I got good news and I got bad news," Pinball said.

Cyrus raised his eyebrows. "Good first."

"I found those cons, Dalton, Hernandez, Jackson."

"And?"

"Bad news is they was all sitting up front, being as they was gonna get out."

"And?" Cyrus narrowed his eyes.

"First two, they took those shots from the cockpit—those two lying over there. The third, that was the one the DEA hit, the guy with his face blowed off back there."

Cyrus sighed and exhaled slowly through pinched lips.

"Hey, Virus, you didn't mean that, did you, about two-bit crackhead?"

"Don't be so sensitive, Pinball. You've heard people call you worse."

"Yeah, but when you dropped that guy, the bullet went wheee . . ." he slid a hand past his head, "where, man, if I'd of hiccuped, I'd be gone."

"Good you didn't hiccup, Pinball. I'd hate to lose such a valuable ally."

"Thanks, Virus. That's all I needed to know."

Cyrus cupped his hands around his mouth to call out to the milling convicts. "Listen up! I need volunteers. Carson City's expecting six men to get off this plane for transfer. They will get what they expect. We've got three. We need three more. I need three volunteers!"

"Don't look at me, pal," Billy Bedlam said, spitting into the aisle. "I'm looking at eight life terms. So I ain't getting off this plane. Not 'til we're in Timbuktu or someplace."

"Pinball here has informed me that the men they're expecting are white," Cyrus said. "That means that most of you here are out of luck, if you were planning to end your excursion in Nevada."

"Oh, man," Baby-O groaned, feeling disappointment now to go with his increasing physical discomfort.

"Now, now, this can't be the first time the color of your skin has put you at a severe disadvantage, my friend. Sit back down."

Baby-O sagged in his seat as Cyrus walked by, looking right and left for volunteers.

"That's it, bro," Baby-O said. "I'm gone. I'm dead in three hours, give or take."

"Hang on, bud," Poe said under his breath. "They're gonna put down in Carson City. I'll get off, pull some coattails fast. This plane'll never leave Carson City."

"Whoo, man, I don't know."

Cyrus strode by. "I need one more. Nobody? All right, we'll take the pilot. When we land, we'll put him in prison blues."

"Hold on," Billy Bedlam said. "What do you mean, the pilot? Who's gonna fly the damn plane? We got places to go!"

"Relax, Billy. We got it covered. Welcome to the machine."

The plane banked into its descent. Cyrus went into the cockpit.

The pilot glanced back. "Carson tower is reporting a helluva sandstorm down there."

"Fine," Cyrus said. "You put her down nice and easy. It'll be like a day at the beach."

Agent Vince Larkin sat hunched over his desk, studying an exercise chart as if it were a State of the Union address. He was falling behind in his schedule. He had thought he'd be in shape to run a marathon by the end of the year, but lately he hadn't been able to keep his weekly mileage up—he should be running fifty miles a week by now, according to the chart, and he ran only twenty last week, eighteen the week before, none in the last three days.

"Hey, Vince?" Ginny walked in. "The plane's on final approach to Carson City."

"Right on time."

"Whatcha reading?"

"Oh, stuff on behavioral patterns." He quickly folded up the charts and went to the closet for his coat. "I'm going over to Vacaville to arrange for the move tomorrow. Wanna come?"

More than anything, she thought. "Nah. Thanks. Paperwork. Bring me some Braren wine— they got a vineyard near there."

"Like I got time."

"Well, sometimes you got time. Any weekend plans?"

He looked at her. Sometimes he couldn't figure her out. "The usual. I'll have one day left, maybe. Pizza, a twelve-pack of Anchor Steam, whatever sports are on."

She studied him as he shrugged into his trench-coat. "Here's a news flash for you, Vince. There's more to life than the smooth and efficient transfer of federal prisoners."

"I'm sure there is. Somewhere out there." He patted her head as he walked by. "I'll pick up that wine for you, if I can."

She sighed as he walked off down the hall. "Somewhere out there is right here," she mumbled. "Wine and me and thou, you idiot."

SEVEN

The C-123 descended through clouds, to outward appearances just another cargo carrier preparing to land and unload. But in this plane, convicts grabbed arms and legs of four bodies—the copilot in the cockpit, three convicts in the main cabin—and dragged them to the rear. Falzon, Bishop, and the other guards were shackled to the mesh walls of the cages in their underwear. Blood was smeared on the floor and walls. The fuselage stank from the brief fire in the seat that gave the Indian superficial burns to his arms; he remained stoically silent and uncomplaining.

The pilot sweated with fear of the future. "What's gonna happen when we land?" he asked again and again whenever Cyrus came in. "You gonna let us go, or kill us, or what?"

"Don't you worry," was Cyrus's repeated reply.

The pilot, now dressed in prison blues, nervously brought the ship down through the swirling sand. Visibility was diminished enough to satisfy Cyrus the Virus that their plan would work. The plane bumped and the wheels squealed on meeting the tarmac.

Two Bureau of Prisons buses awaited arrival of the transferees, scheduled for different destinations, and BOP guards stood with shotguns at the ready, just as others had at departure in Oakland. But there was no extraordinary tension among them; prisoner movements took place all the time.

The plane taxied not quite as close to its assigned stopping point as might have been expected. The visibility could be a suitable excuse. The pilot, prodded by Cyrus, hurried back to join the others assigned to leave. Cameron Poe was among those standing by the exit door.

Cyrus addressed the group, matter-of-factly. "In a couple of hours or so you'll be out of harm's way, either at your Nevada institution or wherever. And just to make sure you don't gab during the trip, Pinball here will prepare you."

Pinball prepared the first men in line, the pilot and an aging con named Kelly. "Okay boys, the bag and gag," he said cheerily. He slapped tape over their mouths and pulled mesh bags down over their heads.

"Not that I don't trust you, boys," Cyrus said. "But let's be honest: you're criminals." He allowed himself a chuckle.

The three "volunteers" had their original bar-code bracelets cut off, to be replaced by the bracelets that had belonged to the dead cons. These were reattached with deft electrical blasts from the taser gun, melding the plastic.

Diamond Dog leaned over to whisper in Cyrus's ear. "What about the rest of the guards?"

"Patience, friend," Cyrus said, not bothering to whisper. "We discard what is not useful to us, retain what is. Certain elements remain useful to us, for the time being."

Cameron Poe looked over at Bishop, chained to the cage. Despite her inelegant position, she held her chin up and met his eyes. Other prisoners ogled her; Poe's look was clearly not lustful, but supportive, pained.

Johnny Twenty-Three saw where Poe's gaze was directed and walked over. "I will fuck her," he said, grinning. "Then I will fuck you. Then I will fuck anybody you're friendly with."

"Just for starters," Poe said evenly, "I suggest you fuck yourself."

"Yo, white boy," Pinball said, grabbing Poe's elbow to turn him around, "your turn." He stretched duct tape across Poe's mouth.

Poe's eyes now caught Baby-O. Baby-O, his watery eyes closed, was hugging himself, rocking back and forth. He wouldn't be able to hang on much longer.

Pinball reached over Poe's head with the mesh bag. Poe shoved him back and ripped the tape off his mouth.

"I'm not going," Poe said.

"What?"

"I'm gonna stay. I don't trust it out there."

"Hey, Cyrus." Pinball kept his eyes on Poe while he motioned to Cyrus. "We got us a mind-changer."

Cyrus ambled over.

"He says he ain't going," Pinball said.

"What's up, friend?"

"I'm staying, that's all."

"I need a reason."

"I got fifteen years left, out of a life-with-parole, and I don't wanna do it. I don't trust those bastards, after all this."

"That's all? Just a minute ago that fifteen years didn't bother you."

Poe shrugged. "Maybe I just don't wanna blow a shot at dirty, naked broads and umbrella drinks."

Cyrus contemplated him, pursing his lips. "What'd you say your name was?"

"Cameron Poe."

Diamond Dog snapped straight. "You're Cameron Poe?"

Poe looked at him.

"I know that name," Pinball said. "I heard it."

"You killed the Giant," Diamond Dog said.

"Who's that?" Billy Bedlam put in.

" 'Giant Carp,' we called him—Heddy Larry. Big, bad mother. You put him down on the tiles, I heard. You shanked him during that riot, I heard. Ain't nobody dared to face the Giant. Hot damn."

"Now," Cyrus said, contemplatively, "why'd you go and do a thing like that, Cameron Poe?"

Poe stared at him for a few seconds. "Maybe he took my strawberry Jell-O."

They stared back, then the two guffawed, joined quickly by Pinball.

"I like you, Cameron Poe," Cyrus said. "You and your friend Baby-O grab one of the guards—your choice—and put that dead cop's prison blues on him."

Poe went down the aisle, pulled up Baby-O by the shirt, and said, "We got a job to do."

"What the fuck?" Baby-O was shivering. "I thought you was gone."

"I'm staying. They're gagging everybody for the bus ride to the pen. We gotta get that agent's clothes."

"I ain't touching that dead bastard."

"Just like undressing a baby. Come on."

Six feet away from where Falzon and Bishop were chained, they began pulling the shoes and then the pants off the corpse of Agent Sims. Baby-O kept his chin tucked into his chest to avoid looking at the damaged head.

"Why you here, bro?" Baby-O asked.

"All taped up and bound like I was gonna be, by the time I made the feds understand what was going on, this plane'd be three states away and you'd be dead. She'd be dead, too." He looked up at Bishop, who was watching them. "You have any idea what'll happen to you if we don't get it stopped?"

"Think about your little girl, Poe," Guard Bishop said. "You got obligations."

"You take your obligations as they come," Poe said. "This first. I gotta live with myself."

Baby-O grabbed a fistful of Poe's shirt. "What good you gonna be dead, bro? You're thinking like you're still a Ranger. You're a convict now, bro. You ain't that guy anymore. You can't do diddly about this shit."

"Well, you never know." Poe took Sims' pants over to Falzon and tossed them over his shoulder. He plucked the photograph of Casey from Falzon's shirt pocket. "Put those pants on, Falzon. Let's say you gave my daughter's picture back. In turn, I just saved your life."

"I ain't taking this dude's shirt off," Baby-O called, standing beside the body, holding the shoes.

"Okay, go sit down. I'll finish."

Poe knelt down and began unbuttoning Sims' shirt. His fingers stopped. They had touched something metallic. He carefully undid one more button. He saw the edge of a tape recorder, the capstans spinning. He blew out slowly through closed lips. He looked up. Bishop was watching.

"Oh! Oh! I got a cramp!" she yelled, doubling over.

That was long enough for Poe to yank the tiny recorder free from its tape, hit "rewind," and slip it into his own pocket.

EIGHT

Members of the ground crew wore cloths over their mouths and noses, and goggles, to operate in the blowing sand. A fuel truck arrived with a boom for pumping into the valve on the top of the wing. The driver connected the nozzle to the socket and began pumping jet fuel for the turboprops into the tanks.

The rear ramp lowered and a guard stepped off the C-123 into the sandstorm. The "guard" was Cyrus the Virus, in a blue jumpsuit and black jackboots that didn't fit him exactly, with a Marshal cap over his long hair and his face obscured by a blue bandanna and sunglasses. He was followed by Billy Bedlam and Johnny Twenty-Three similarly dressed in what, had the weather been clear, would have been recognized as ill-fitting uniforms. In this weather they looked real enough.

A marshal from the ground unit came up. "Hi.

I'm Starkey, heading up this unit. Heard you had a problem up there."

"Yeah," Cyrus said, in a husky voice. "Rough bunch, got rowdy. A bunch of critters that was spitters and shitters. Had to bag 'em and gag 'em. But they're okay now, as you can see."

The "prisoners," including the flight crew, filed down the ramp.

The BOP guards began offloading their buses. First off was a convict who nodded discreetly to Cyrus, who patted him down. "Swamp Thing," Cyrus mumbled. He felt Swamp Thing quiver with a chuckle.

Inside the plane, Falzon, bound and gagged, rigged up like the other "prisoners," was about to head down the ramp.

Poe grabbed him and threw him up against the wall. "My daughter's picture! Where's my daughter's picture, peckerhead?" While Falzon looked at him wild-eyed, Poe slid the recorder into Falzon's shirt and hit "play." Then Poe shoved him down the ramp, so that he exited stumbling.

Falzon regained his balance as a guard grabbed his arm to scan the bar code on his wrist band. The tape recorder was playing, but the sound was obscured by the wind and the rumbling of trucks and voices around the plane. The weather was beginning to clear in the west; not soon enough for his short trip to the BOP buses.

Johnny Twenty-Three, another "guard," awaited the next transfer from Carson City—a six-foot-six ex-football player with a Mohawk strip of hair down the center of his head named Conrad. Conrad, who'd just turned thirty, an age he considered to be the Age of Pain, held up his cuffed hands to Johnny.

"You wanna know my favorite fantasy? Killing every cop in the system, then fucking them. Or do I have that backwards?"

Johnny shoved him forward up the ramp.

Once in the plane, Conrad did a double take at the sight of Pinball. He looked around, confused, seeing other faces. Then it dawned on him.

"Great Holy Mary motherfucker! Out of the fire and into the freebird!" Conrad slapped his thigh and hee-hawed.

Next out of the BOP bus was a skinny Latin boy, in a hair net and wearing mascara; a boy with high cheekbones and full lips and widening hips—a recipient of hormone shots that had not yet turned him feminine enough. He waltzed up to Johnny Twenty-Three for the pat-down.

"Hello, baby," he cooed. "You can be the rose of my Spanish Harlem, if you've a mind. They call me 'Sally Can't Dance.' Why? Guess, sweetie."

"Get your fat ass on the plane," Johnny barked.

"Now, now, honey. This fat ass could be yours, you play your cards."

In the plane, Swamp Thing climbed into the cockpit and slid behind the pilot's controls. Beside him, Pinball finished changing into a guard's uniform, putting on goggles and a bandanna and wearing the pen clip around his neck.

Swamp Thing unscrewed a small device, like a radio, from the control panel. To that he attached a little nine-volt battery, twisting together slender wires. He handed the device to Pinball. "Go get 'em, son."

Pinball tossed the device in his hand, smiled broadly, and headed for the rear ramp.

When he exited into the clearing weather and diminishing wind, he saw Falzon in the arms of guards a few yards away, acting spastic, swinging his head, throwing his body around. "He's just bonkers!" Pinball hollered to nobody in particular. He walked away from the plane and buses, all the way to the other side of the airport.

He approached a hangar with a sign painted on it that read: "Uncle Bob's Grand Canyon Tours." Outside the hangar was a six-seat twin-engine turboprop with a picture of Uncle Bob painted on the fuselage.

Uncle Bob was wearing a gaudy rayon Hawaiian short-sleeved shirt and a white pith helmet. Two parents with a little girl between them were filling out forms as a crewman loaded luggage into the nose.

Uncle Bob was yelling over the wind: "Don't worry about this little bit of weather! No problem! Only goes up fifty feet!"

Pinball waited twenty yards away until the crewman left to get more luggage. Then he walked over, behind the yelling Uncle Bob, tossed the small radio device into the luggage compartment, made an abrupt U-turn, and kept on walking.

Back in the area of the C-123, a man stepped out of the bus and gave Cyrus the slightest of smiles as he was patted down. Lean, fit, deeply tanned, with perfect posture, he was one of the youngest of the group, and one of the smallest, but still the most confident of them all.

"You look a lot like Francisco Cindino," Cyrus said. He turned to marshal chief Starkey. "Is that it?"

"One more." He tapped his pen on the clipboard manifest. "A late arrival. Name is Garland Greene. Coming up now."

He gestured back to where a high-security prison van entered the tarmac from an access road and pulled up next to the plane. Two deputies carrying submachine guns stepped from the front, two more from the side. Then a solitary prisoner stepped gingerly off. A thin, pale, frail-looking man in his early thirties, he wore complete restraints. The chains on him seemed outsized as he clanked along with small shuffling steps.

"This ought to be interesting," said Cyrus the Virus, as he watched Garland Greene being led up the ramp.

The "prisoners" from the C-123, taped and bagged, were led onto their bus. Cyrus watched edgily as they climbed up one by one. He walked over to the fuel truck. "What's taking so long?" he called up to the fuel jockey.

"Pardon?" the man removed one side of his ear protectors.

"How long? We're on a tight schedule."

"Be about another ten minutes or so," the man answered.

"Well, squeeze it, friend, okay?"

The man saluted and replaced his ear protectors.

The two guards inventorying in minute detail the newly evacuated cell at Vacaville Prison were reasonably well trained but not widely experienced; they seldom found anything of interest in these searches.

"Loose shelf screw," Guard Garner reported to Guard Renfro, who noted it on a clipboard. Garner ran his fingers around a mirror. "Right corner of mirror bent." He moved on. "Weapon-sharpening mark on north wall."

They both chuckled; there was an absolute taboo on anything resembling, or that could be made to resemble, a weapon; everybody had a weapon; everybody knew about it.

"A chip on . . . Hey, wait. What's this?"

Garner dropped to his knees. He had found a crumbling section of concrete in the lower wall, a place so painstakingly restored that the difference from the solid concrete was virtually invisible. He had found it by testing the wall with his fingers. He pushed at the concrete, and it began to break away.

Renfro dropped to his knees beside him. With pen tips they began to chip at more of the wall. A hole appeared, then widened to reveal a small cache of stuff.

Garner began tugging things out with his fingers. He brought out folded papers, a nail file, a small notebook. Behind those things the hole was wider still, larger things could be seen. "Oh man, we gotta show some of this stuff, right now." He gathered a few of the things and headed out in the hall where the surveillance monitors were.

He stood and waited, not long. The supervisor's voice came over the intercom.

"What is it, Garner?"

"Sir, we found a hiding place."

In the supervisor's office, watching the monitor with him was Vince Larkin. They watched the monitor as Garner unfurled a rolled-up sheet of vellum paper with airplane specs printed on it.

"Whose cell is that?" Larkin asked.

"Grissom," the supervisor said. "Cyrus Grissom. You ever heard of Cyrus the Virus?"

"Oh no—" Larkin ran out the door.

"What is it?" the supervisor yelled after him.

"We got him!" Larkin called back as he raced down the corridor.

The last prisoner was led to his seat by a jumpy guard who was aware that the others on the plane were watching in awe.

"Jesus, Mary, and Katmandu," Baby-O whispered. "That's Garland Greene, bro."

"Garland Greene, the Marietta Mangler?" Poe said.

"Yup. That's the skinny little guy butchered thirty people all along the eastern seaboard, made the Manson family look like the Partridge family."

"Fits right in on this flight."

"You got that right, bro. Shoo, that sucker don't look like he could bend a hairpin, and he did all those people."

· · ·

To begin with, before the door was closed to the noise of the airport, the duct-taped "prisoner" guards on the BOP bus sat immobilized. But as soon as the door closed and the bus began to roll away from the plane, they began to thrash about, groaning and grunting.

The BOP guards, supposing they were just being obstreperous, began to swat them with their billy clubs to quiet them down. The grunting and thrashing persisted, so did the clubbing, until Falzon took a hard one on the noggin and slumped over. Suddenly the noise stopped.

And then the voices came from Falzon's chest:

". . . Shoot him . . . do it," came Bishop's voice. "Quiet, sweetheart," came the voice of Cyrus. "I think you better drop the gun, cowboy," came Poe's.

The guards looked confused, looking for the source of the voices.

There was the sound of a shot, followed by: "How's that for control, asshole?" The voice of Agent Sims.

A guard stared briefly at the slumped Falzon, his eyes wandering down from his taped mouth. Then he dove on him to tear open Falzon's shirt, revealing the tape recorder.

". . . You got a chance, if you give me that gun. . . ."

"Holy shit!" the guard yelled. "We got a spy or a rat or an agent or some damned thing! This fucking guy is wired—backwards!"

Larkin was on his hands and knees, reaching an arm's length into the hole in the wall of the cell. Guards Garner and Renfro watched over his shoulder. He extracted a book entitled *Volatile Chemical Compounds,* and then one entitled *Fairchild C-123K Provider Service Manual.*

He thumbed through the manual briefly, seeing instructions and specifications. He reached in again and pulled out a passenger manifest for their flight. "Oh, my." He pulled out a pile of letters, and a tin box.

"Here's one that was with the earlier stuff," Garner said, handing him a letter on formal stationery.

"Bogotá, Colombia?" Larkin said, scanning it. "Looks like from a law firm. Gotta find somebody who reads Spanish."

Garner picked up an item from the growing pile. "Hey, check this out. Pretty creepy."

It was a small copy of the painting "The Last Supper." Except that in this version most of the participants' eyes had been punched out.

Larkin studied it. Then it dawned on him. He lay the picture atop the letter from Colombia, maneuvered it around, and saw that, when it was lined up a certain way, single distinct letters appeared in the eyeholes.

"Wow," he said, taking a pen and small pad out of his pocket. He uncapped the pen with his teeth and began recording the eyehole letters on his pad.

Johnny Twenty-Three (Danny Trejo), atop the control tower at the Death Valley rendezvous, signals to the convicts an approach of a government convoy.

The hijacked C-123 "Provider" cargo plane comes in for a landing at Carson City, where transfers of bogus "convicts"—captured guards—will be made.

U.S. Marshal Vance Larkin (John Cusack) tries to communicate with the hijackers aboard the C-123.

DEA Agent Duncan Malloy (Colm Meaney) arrives to supervise the planting of an undercover agent amid the convicts about to board the transfer flight.

Convict and former U.S. Army Ranger Cameron Poe (Nicolas Cage), who this day is scheduled for release, leaves a prison bus to board the ill-fated transfer flight.

Convict "Swamp Thing" tows the prisoners' plane toward the Death Valley runway as their supposed escape plane explodes in the background.

Cameron Poe awaits his fate and the fate of the rest of the convicts aboard the C-123.

A maximum-security prison bus is escorted out of San Quentin for the trip to the transport plane.

In the midst of a sandstorm in Carson City, U.S. Marshal Starkey, surrounded by convicts disguised as guards, supervises the transfer of prisoners from the plane he doesn't know has been hijacked.

Lawmen advance through the airplane junkyard at Lerner Airfield in Death Valley in a firefight with the convicts who hijacked the C-123.

Captured guards, dressed up like convicts, are led out of the C-123 by convicts, dressed up like guards, who have hijacked the plane. A sandstorm helps conceal identities.

Convict leader Cyrus "the Virus" Grissom (John Malkovich)
—murderer, kidnapper, psychologist—steps out of his onboard
cage after being freed by the plane's hijackers.

Swamp Thing (M. C. Gainey) with Cyrus "the Virus," who
is wearing the uniform of guard Falzon and worrying about
who is the "rat" among the convicts.

Cyrus "the Virus" gathers other convicts around at the rendezvous site to question them on the possible "rat" among them.

As law-enforcement officers approach the airfield in Death Valley, Cyrus "the Virus" prepares to launch an ambush.

NINE

"Uh-oh," Diamond Dog said to Johnny Twenty-Three as they watched out the window of the Provider.

"Uh-oh," Johnny echoed.

What they were watching was the BOP bus as it rolled slowly away across the tarmac. What they saw now was that the bus stopped. They couldn't see anything through the blackened and barred windows of the bus. But there was no good-news reason for the bus to stop.

They watched, holding their breath. The bus began to roll again, even slower, though, than before.

"It's going, it's going," Johnny said.

"I hope so, I hope so," Diamond Dog said.

Inside the bus, belying the slow, smooth course it seemed to have resumed, there was chaos. The duct tape had been removed, and all mouths were yammering at once, everybody wildly pointing and demonstrating at once.

"We've got a situation here, sir!" a bus guard shouted into the CB radio. "The plane has been taken over! Repeat: The plane has been taken over!"

Before he finished the message, airport security men were grabbing flak jackets and shotguns and M-16s and racing out to emergency vans. Within seconds, vans were squealing into turns, heading out on the tarmac.

In the U.S. Marshal car still remaining next to the C-123, Starkey received the news over his radio.

"Those guards ain't guards," said the voice of the BOP man in the control center. "They're cons. Stall 'em."

"Christ," Starkey responded. "How we supposed to do that?"

"You gotta come up with something. You gotta do something bold. But watch your ass."

"Yeah, sure. Go out there to those lifers and stall 'em, and watch my ass. Okay, I'm on it."

Starkey's throat was dry and his skin clammy as he stepped out of the car and started toward the Provider. He was trying to stroll, but he worried that his hesitant step might look more like a limp.

Cyrus, standing near the refueling hose, watched him approaching. "Hi there, Starkey," he said.

"Hi there. How's it going? What'd you say your name was?"

"Uh, Hazelnut. Fine, fine. Pumping away."

"Almost ready?"

"Won't be long now. Couple of minutes."

Starkey nodded and tried to swallow and stay casual. Out of the corner of his eye he saw the two security vans speeding their way.

Cyrus noticed his glance and followed his eyes.

Starkey noticed Cyrus noticing his look and reached to unhook the safety strap on his holster.

But Cyrus fired first. The last thing Starkey saw, as he staggered back with a hole in his head, was the fuel jockey on the wing, with his ear covers on, watching his nozzle, oblivious to events.

Inside the Provider, everybody heard the shot.

Pinball, walking back from his delivery of the radio device to the sightseeing plane at the other side of the airport, heard it too. And he saw the speeding vans. "Shit!" he spouted as he began to sprint toward the plane.

The motors were revving. The rear ramp was already going up. "Hold it! Hold it!" Pinball yelled as he ran. "Wait, you bastards!"

Swamp Thing, visions of defoliation runs in Viet Nam, and night deliveries for the CIA's Air

America operations all over Southeast Asia dancing in his head, advanced the throttles. The plane lurched forward. The fuel jockey tumbled off the wing. The fuel hose pulled taut in its socket, then snapped. The plane turned a sharp ninety degrees and headed for the runway.

"You prick bastards, wait!" Pinball ran beside the plane, reaching for a hold.

Behind him, the vans screeched to a halt, security men jumped out and aimed their semiautomatic rifles.

"Haw!" sang Swamp Thing at the controls. "This baby's gonna fly, fly, fly away with me!"

"What the hell are you doing?" came the voice of the air-traffic controller over the radio.

"Flying my plane!" Swamp Thing sang.

"We've got three planes lined up coming in on that runway! Back off! Back off!"

"Up yours! Nobody on this aircraft gives a flying fuck! We're off into the wild blue yonder, headed upstairs to the great beyond, beyond yonder. Over and out, you land crabs! Haw!"

He straightened out the plane on the runway and pushed the throttles all the way forward. The engines roared, the plane surged forward and was quickly airborne.

"Sweet, huh?" Swamp Thing said to Cyrus.

Airport security men standing below let their ri-

fles droop as they gaped into the sky. The plane
became smaller, became a dot.

On his knees, Vince Larkin carefully lined up the
vacant eyes over the letters and began to write on
his pad: "ME ETC ARSON C IT Y"

He sat back and looked at the eyes and the letters. "What the hell does that mean?" he muttered.
" 'Me etc?' "

Guards Garner and Renfro, looking over his
shoulder, shook their heads. He leaned forward
again and played with the letters, arranging them.
Suddenly he saw it. "MEET CARSON CITY."

"Stay here!" he barked, springing to his feet.
"Don't touch anything!"

Larkin ran out of the cell.

Renfro and Garner stared at "The Last Supper"
with its punched-out eyes filled with letters.

"Things are strange," Renfro said.

"Weird things going on," Garner said. He
picked up the tin box Larkin had pulled out of the
hole. It had a picture of an old Ford trimotor airplane on the lid. "I'm curious. You curious?"

"You heard him, Garner. Don't fuck with that."

"He said don't touch anything. This has already
been touched. Anyway, he should have checked this
before he left. We got a duty."

Garner lifted the lid and had the briefest glimpse of the trigger and detonator cap before the box exploded.

The fireball flashed into the hallway behind Larkin. He was thrown forward. He scrambled to his feet and headed back toward the smoke and rubble.

Larkin and Devers rushed down the corridor toward the marshals' offices at Oakland Airport, Ginny following, her French heels clattering on the tiles.

"That plane was carrying a thousand years worth of murders and psychopaths to Feltham."

"Still carrying a thousand years," Larkin said grimly. "We just don't know where to."

"Be nice if they could just stay up there forever, wouldn't it?"

Agent Duncan Malloy came around the corner and charged toward them. "What the fuck happened? My agent? What happened to Sims?"

They all stopped. Duncan looked from face to face.

"They killed him, Duncan," Devers said.

Duncan sagged back against the wall, stunned. "Six years ago," he said vacantly, "William Sims came to me and said he wanted to be a soldier in the war against drugs." Suddenly he snapped back.

"You got my man killed, you little shit!" He lunged at Larkin.

Devers stepped between them, stopping Duncan with a forearm.

"He brought a gun on board," Larkin said gruffly. "He pulled a pistol on them, shot a man, and got shot."

"Damn right! Damn right he did!" Duncan leaned against Devers' arm, his hands clenched. "He was doing his job!"

"His job was not to compromise the safety of my men," Larkin said. "Those guards were doing their job, too, unarmed."

"So? So? Your men were incompetent! A bunch of thugs in chains and cages whipped their asses! And got my man killed!"

"Cool it, both of you!" Devers barked. "Duncan, I'll have you cuffed if I have to!"

There were a few seconds of heavy breathing and fierce stares. Then they relaxed a bit.

"Okay, okay," Duncan said, pushing air with his hands. "What's the plan? What's the backup? You gotta have a backup plan."

"I'm working on it," Larkin said. "This situation couldn't have been anticipated."

"Bullshit! It's—"

"Whatever they planned, however clever it was, they've had incredible luck. The plan worked better than they could ever have dreamed. We could contemplate how desperate they were, not how lucky."

"Well, you'd better start contemplating now, because this situation ain't gonna stay this fucked up. These guys are gonna pay. Everybody's gonna pay!"

"Cool it, Duncan," Devers said. "Let's go to work."

"Francisco Cindino," Cyrus the Virus said, "meet Diamond Dog, my man."

They nodded at each other, steadying themselves as the plane climbed and banked.

Cindino fixed Cyrus with his eyes. "This has not been exactly the most skillful execution of a plan, Mr. Grissom."

"No, that's true. Something happened, got in the way."

"I suggest you determine what that 'something' was."

"Of course, Francisco, we're working on it."

"You think we fucked up in some way?" Diamond Dog said, narrowing his eyes. "You blaming us?"

Francisco turned his head slowly toward Diamond Dog. "I don't think in terms of blame. That's a waste of time. I think in terms of efficient operation. I think in terms of getting things done."

"We're getting it done."

"We'll see. It's not done yet."

Up the aisle, Guard Bishop, no longer chained but now confined in a cage, put her face to the bars. "Hey, Poe? What's up?"

"How you doing, Bishop?"

"Living out all my fantasies, Poe."

"You got a family?"

"I got a cat. I had a husband. He didn't like the cat. I had to make a choice. In five years, the cat never got drunk and embarrassed me in front of my friends; my husband never purred. So it wasn't a tough choice at all."

"Hmm."

"Tell me something, Poe. You really offed that man because of a beef over Jell-O?"

"He was gonna brain me with a club. It was self-defense."

"They know you did it?"

"Maybe yes, maybe no. But they moved me to Quentin, so I was far as I could be from home."

"That's the way they do," she said.

Poe's attention was drawn to the rear, where Cyrus and Diamond Dog contemplated the chained and bagged Garland Greene.

"What are we supposed to do with him?" Dog said, as if Greene couldn't hear.

"This is no way to treat a national treasure,"

Cyrus said, pulling the mesh bag off Garland's head and directing a con to open the locks. "Love your work, friend."

Garland responded with a bloodless smile.

"Where's Pinball?" Cyrus said. "I want him to meet you."

Poe took a seat next to Baby-O, who was groaning softly.

"I got the chucks, bro," Baby-O said. "The chuck-horrors coming on hard."

"Hang in, bro. Hold on tight. We'll get you taken care of. You just gotta hang on."

Billy Bedlam sauntered up. "Hey, Poe, let's let bygones be, okay?"

Poe looked up at him.

"So, you were in the Q, right?" Bedlam said.

"Yeah."

"And you're a lifer, I hear you say?"

"Fifteen left of it, you heard me say."

"Fifteen of a life, right." He paused, looked away and pursed his lips, then looked back. "Lifers are all confined to North Block, aren't they?"

"I wouldn't know about all lifers."

"But you."

"Yeah."

"I was on North Block. I don't know you."

"There were a hundred and sixty men on North Block, and I didn't wanna know one hundred and fifty-nine of them. That must've included you."

Bedlam grunted and started away, then swung back. "We will tango, Poe."

"Really?"

"I don't trust you. I don't like your face. We will tango."

"I don't dance."

TEN

Diamond Dog stepped carefully into the cockpit, where Cyrus and Cindino were conferring with Swamp Thing.

"This old buzzard ain't got no kick," Swamp Thing said, wiggling the yoke. "Let me at those engines for a day or two, we'll add fifty knots."

"Excuse me," said Diamond Dog. Their heads swiveled toward him. "Pinball didn't make it."

"What do you mean?" Cyrus said.

"He ain't on the plane. He was running along. We took off."

"We've lost the element of surprise!" Cindino whined.

"He won't rat us out," Dog growled.

"Calm down, Francisco," Cyrus said. "I've got contingencies on contingencies. That's why your father chose me, friend. I'm your guy. I'll miss Pinball, but they couldn't beat anything out of him with a lamppost. And he doesn't know anything anyway. He barely knows where he's at from time to time, and where he's at now is not here, so he's got nothing to tell. So not to worry."

Cameron Poe stood in the doorway.

"What do you want?" Diamond Dog said.

"If I'm in this, I want to know the plan."

They were interrupted by the radio crackling to life.

"Cyrus? Cyrus Grissom? You copy? Put your ears on, Cyrus. This is United States Marshal Vince Larkin, here at Oakland with Duncan Malloy of DEA."

Swamp Thing lifted the mike and handed it to Cyrus.

"Hello, Agent Malloy," Cyrus cooed. "Sorry about your associate. There is really nothing sadder than the sight of a grown man pissing himself."

"Listen here, you fucking animal!" came Malloy's voice.

Cyrus closed his eyes and smiled, savoring Malloy's rage.

". . . Grissom, you puny punk! When I get through with you, you'll be begging for the chair!"

There was a silence. Cyrus waited a few seconds, then said calmly, "I don't think I like him, Marshal Larkin. If he speaks again, this conversation is terminated."

"Okay, okay, he's off," Larkin said. "Let's talk."

"Fine. I will speak to you. Here are the rules: I get one question, you get one question."

"Let's not play games, Grissom."

"The game of life and death, Larkin. You in?"

Larkin sighed. "Okay. What's your question, Cyrus?"

"Your bulls got onto us in Carson City. How?"

Malloy jumped in. "One of the guards had a—"

"—a heart attack," Larkin concluded the sentence. "He faked a heart attack, and we had to remove his restraints, the tape."

"And your question?" Cyrus said.

"What's your destination?"

"Disneyland."

"Come on, Cyrus, we had a deal."

"You lied, Vince. There was no heart attack. Good-bye, Agent Larkin."

Larkin listened to the empty static for a few seconds, then turned to Ginny. "Brief the FAA. Get them to direct all air traffic away from that area of the Southwest. Let's find out how many gang affiliations we've got on board, who belongs to what. I want to know everything."

"You got it, Vince." She trotted out.

"They refueled in Carson City," he said to Malloy. "So the next possible landing is within a radius of about 102 minutes of flight time from Carson City."

"How do you know that?"

"We refuel only enough to take the plane to its next destination. It's a . . . security measure." He winced at his own words.

"Security!" Malloy scoffed. "You talk security!"

Air-traffic control came on the radio. "Larkin, transponder indicates they're heading southeast toward Arizona."

"Roger, ATC."

"I want a chopper!" Malloy bellowed. "Make that three! Armed, maybe Cobras, something fast enough to keep up with that slowpoke plane. I don't care if it's Army, Navy, National Guard, whatever."

"Easy, Malloy," Larkin said. "We don't want to spook people."

"Spook hell. I want to shoot the bastards down!"

Poe sat with Baby-O, occasionally patting his hand.

Diamond Dog stopped in the aisle. "What's really on your brain, Giantkiller?"

"Why's a black militant taking orders from a white boy on this expedition?"

"Cyrus is a means to an end, my boy. I'm in for

life. If Cyrus the Virus has figured a way out, I can play house-nigger until we get where we're going."

"Then what happens?"

"Darkness falls, my man. The Day of the Dog begins." Dog walked away, cackling.

"What was that about?" Baby-O asked.

"The freaks managed to take this over," Poe said, "and they got us stuck right in the middle. I'm trying to make the middle a little hot, stir things up. Maybe we'll find a crack."

"I could stand a little heat, bro. I'm freezing."

"Hang on, bro. We'll bring it home."

The group of marshals sat around a conference table.

"Here's his jacket," Larkin said, passing out files. "Cameron Poe. Army Ranger, highly decorated, tough as nails. A hell-raiser as a kid, nothing later, until the manslaughter—which in my opinion is a little doubtful. But anyway, he may be the key."

"Explain just why any of this matters," Malloy said, grumpily.

"Fact one: You've got a planeful of thieves, rapists, killers, and this guy Poe. He's on an involuntary manslaughter rap, not gang-affiliated in the joint, on his way out, just hitching a ride home. Fact two: He has a chance to get off the plane but doesn't. Fact three: Our guard Falzon says Cameron Poe planted Sims' tape recorder on him. Why this matters is, I think we've got an ally on board."

"What speculative horseshit."

"Listen, Malloy, we got a job to do. Grow up."

"Guys, guys," Devers broke in, "let's ease up on that."

"The guy's a murderer," Malloy said.

"A drunken brawl, defending his wife," Larkin said.

"Fucking animal."

"Oh? You know what Dostoevsky said after visiting a Russian jail? 'The degree of civilization in a society can be judged by observing its prisoners.' "

"Oh yeah? Well, take a look at what we got on that plane—and he's with them!"

"Guys, guys," Devers said, "the only issue here is how that plane is gonna be corralled."

"Shoot the sucker down," Malloy said.

"Not the DEA's jurisdiction," Larkin said.

"It became DEA the second a DEA agent was murdered, buster. I'm authorized to bring his killers to justice, using, and I quote, 'all necessary means.' "

"Your necessary is not necessarily our necessary."

"Well, Vince," Devers broke in, "this is a drastic situation."

"Aw, no, boss," Larkin moaned, "you're not considering that seriously. My men are up there."

"Every one of them signed a no-hostage waiver. They know the drill."

They heard the whup-whup of helicopter blades, and all looked up as if they could see them through the ceiling.

"About time," Malloy said.

"What the hell's going on, skip?" Larkin asked.

"Attack choppers, Vince. We're going after those cons."

They filed out into the corridor. Malloy hurried ahead.

"Skip, this is a bad idea," Larkin continued, quietly. "Malloy is too hot to be trusted. His agent was killed, he wants revenge. You hearing me, chief?"

Devers ignored him. Larkin trotted ahead to confront Malloy. He jumped in front of him.

"Listen! You're going to kill six innocent people up there. You and Grissom are a lot alike: Both like the soft white underbelly of the kill."

"Not now, Larkin, get away."

"You both got the taste," Larkin went on, not letting him pass. "He dreams about it from his cell; you dream about it in your Corvette. You've got a hard-on right now, thinking about it. Am I right? Huh?"

"You little bastard, I'd kill you too, if I . . . never mind."

"But only in the line of duty, right, Malloy?"

Malloy swept him aside, kicked open the doors, and stepped out into the sunshine where on the tarmac a four-man Huey and two two-man Cobras sat, their blades thumping around, waiting to take off.

They followed him out. Malloy turned to Larkin. "Your work is done, Marshal. Bug off."

Devers slid into the Huey with another marshal. Then Malloy got in.

"Sorry, filled," Malloy said, as Larkin moved for the door.

"Sir! Please. . . ." Larkin pleaded to Devers.

"Go back to your office, Vince," Devers said, gently. "And don't worry. No one here's gonna do anything foolish."

Larkin backed off, stunned to silence, and watched the choppers lift off and bank away.

Cyrus spread a sectional aeronautical chart out on the seat in front of Poe and tapped his finger on an area at the California-Nevada border.

"Lerner Airfield, Cameron Poe. Right smack in the middle of nowhere at all. That's Death Valley. Our rendezvous spot. Near to an hour, as the crow flies, from anything like authority."

Cyrus picked up the intercom mike. "Gentlemen of the main cabin, listen up. In some five hours' time, we will be over the shores of Mexico. That, for those of you who don't know, is outside of the United States. But first we will have to change aircraft. That is all arranged. Thank you, and have a nice day."

He clicked off the intercom and leaned over Swamp Thing. "What's our ETA, friend?"

Swamp Thing watched an amber light on the control panel and frowned. "At 230 miles per hour, round about seventy-one minutes. Problem is, we're not doing 230. We're dragging, at 205. What that light shows is the landing gear ain't up proper. We're gonna be late."

"The gear won't retract?"

"Evidently. This old buzzard's got some bugs to work out. Let me at that gear a couple hours, it'll slide smooth as silk."

"This is unacceptable," Cindino said.

Cyrus turned to Diamond Dog. "Check it out."

"What do I know about a landing gear?"

"We'll find out if you're a good learner," Cyrus said.

The waiting room in the Nevada penitentiary was not a fun place under ordinary circumstances. Today, though, there was at least a representation of gaiety. Both Tricia Poe and her seven-year-old daughter, Casey, were wearing bright gingham dresses and had with them presents brightly wrapped in yellow and green paper. Casey was putting the finishing crayon touches on a cardboard sign: "Welcome Home Daddy!"

"It's beautiful," Tricia said to Casey, who was fretting with imperfections. "Your daddy will love it. Don't worry."

"But I've never *seen* him, and what if he doesn't?"

"Trust me, honey, it's going to be his favorite thing of all."

"You think so?"

"I know so."

"Mrs. Poe?"

She turned to see a dour man in a brown suit. "Yes?"

"My name's Grant, Bureau of Prisons. There's been a slight hitch on your husband's flight."

"A hitch?"

"What's a hitch, Mommy?"

"Just a little problem, Mrs. Poe. We're working to correct it. Meanwhile, your presence has been requested in Oakland. We have air transportation for you. If you'll just follow me." He turned and beckoned them.

They gathered up their things quickly and followed.

"What's a hitch, Mommy? What's a little problem mean?"

"It means your daddy will be a little late, I guess. But everything will be okay. We have to take a little plane ride first."

"Just like Daddy."

"Yup."

ELEVEN

A fierce blast of wind knocked Diamond Dog back as soon as he opened the front floor hatch, and he wasn't about to step closer.

"I ain't goin' in there, Poe!" he called over the roar of the wind, shaking his head rapidly.

"It's just the passageway under the floor. The wind's because the wheel bay is open. It won't be so bad once we drop down there out of the draft."

He slid down the hatch, and Diamond Dog dutifully followed. It was a little calmer there, though they could still hear the wind. They edged through the freight compartment, passing the stacks of prisoners' metal banker's boxes.

"Well, what do you know," Dog said, emitting a low whistle. "They got all our shit down here."

"Yeah." Poe found himself scanning the stack

for his own, and found it. His box had Baby-O's yellow happy-face sticker on it, and he smiled back.

At the end of the compartment, Poe opened the hatch to the wheel bay and was immediately whipped by the wind. The landing-gear doors were partially open.

Poe dropped to his hands and knees and crawled to the center wheel bay and looked in. He recoiled, bumping into Diamond Dog.

"Oof," Diamond Dog said.

"Judas Priest!" Poe said. "There he is!"

"Who?" Diamond Dog slid up beside Poe and looked. "Well, I'll be. So that's where Pinball was all along. He sure ain't gonna rat us out."

"Not likely," Poe said.

"You gotta cut him loose," Dog said.

"Me?"

"You can't leave him in there, squooshed like that. He's slowing us down."

"Cyrus gave you this job."

"Well, I'm outta here." Dog backed away.

Poe looked down at the contorted face of the dead and frozen Pinball. He had evidently grabbed whatever he could when the plane was taxiing, which in this case was the landing gear, and hoisted himself aboard. The gear pinned him in.

Down through the breaks in the clouds Poe

could see the sprawl of a modest-sized city. Studying Pinball's body, he noticed a chain around his neck. He flattened himself on the floor and slid forward, tipping slightly into the opening, far enough to reach the chain, on the end of which was a thick marking pen. As the wind whipped around him, Poe painstakingly wrote on Pinball's T-shirt:

"TO V LARKIN. US MARSHAL SERV. DEST LERNER AIRFIELD. RENDEZVOUS."

Pinball's right arm and leg were twisted around the gear. Poe reached to push them off, but they had stiffened and were unyielding. He pulled himself back and switched to a sitting position, dangling his legs. He kicked at the body again and again. Pinball didn't budge.

"You done, man?" Diamond Dog was crawling back.

"I thought you split."

"Scarier to go up there if this ain't done. Give him a good one."

Poe swung a mighty kick, and Pinball was sprung free and fell. But Poe's momentum took him off the edge and he fell himself into the bay, where he clung to the gear against the tearing of the wind. Pinball spun away downward and became a dot against the landscape.

"Come on, fool!" Dog yelled, reaching down. "Grab ahold!"

They clasped each other's wrists, and it took the full strength of both strong men to bring Poe back inside the aircraft.

"That was a dang fool thing to do," Dog said, massaging his wrist.

Far down below, on a Fresno street, a Buick station wagon pulled out of a car wash, turning into the lane behind a livestock trailer. Almost immediately, a wad of bird droppings spattered on the windshield.

"See that, see that, Maude?" said the driver. "Fifty years I been driving, and it never fails. First minute out of a car wash and some pigeon shits on my car."

"Now, Paw, some say that's good luck."

"Well, I could use some."

At that moment, Pinball's corpse crashed onto the hood, and two seconds later the Buick ran into the rear of the livestock trailer.

Poe returned to his seat next to Baby-O, exhausted. Baby-O was snoozing, for which Poe was grateful.

"Yo, you." Billy Bedlam walked up.

"What now?"

"You remember a big bull in North Block, name

of Victor Lomas? Warden fired him on account of he was gettin' regular head from a nigger con called Lulu."

"Can't say's I do."

"Really? 'Cause it was a big deal on North Block at the time. A scandal. And you don't remember?"

"Like I said." Poe let his eyes close.

"Maybe you ain't really from North Block."

Poe's eyes popped open. "Maybe you should back off, pal. Because my patience is running low. I wouldn't want to put your nose into your brain, like I done a time or two."

Bedlam backed away, waggling a finger. "I'm gonna remember that, Poe."

"I hope you do."

Diamond Dog came by, now wearing a pair of wraparound sunglasses.

"Where'd you get the rims?" Bedlam asked.

"From the stash of our stuff, down in the luggage compartment. There's a shitload of stuff, man."

"Really?"

"I'm Vince Larkin," he said to Tricia Poe, reaching out his hand to shake hers. "And this must be Casey?"

"I'm Casey Poe," she said. "I'm seven."

"Apologize for the inconvenience, Mrs. Poe."

Over coffee, while Casey colored at his desk, Larkin told her the story in concise outline.

"I guess what I'm trying to figure out is why he stayed on the aircraft," Larkin said. "If he is, in fact, trying to stop these guys."

"Well, he certainly isn't one of them, if you still have any doubts about that."

"I don't, really. It wouldn't fit, either his character or the circumstances."

She sipped her coffee. "Cameron is one of the toughest men you could meet. I guess you know that. And he's got a real problem with injustice. Including what's been done to him. But what's been done to him hasn't changed his sense of what's right and wrong."

"Well, that'd be a credit to him, all right."

"He isn't afraid to stand up for what's right, no matter what the odds."

"You got that right, Mrs. Poe. That's what I'm counting on."

She thought for a moment, staring into her cup. "Maybe he was afraid of coming home."

"Pardon?"

"You know," she looked up at him. "Just that he was going to see me again after all these years, and see his daughter for the first time. Maybe he was afraid he couldn't measure up. Maybe he was afraid of living on the outside again after all these years."

"Mrs. Poe," he reached across and tapped her hand. "I think every inmate would have some of those fears. But your husband, there's nothing to suggest that those fears could dominate him. I don't think that's why he stayed on that aircraft."

"Vince?" Ginny stuck her head in. "Call on the law line."

Larkin walked over and picked up the special phone. "Larkin."

"This is Ned Grasso, a sheriff here in Fresno. We got a situation here with a corpse that fell out of the sky onto a Buick. The case's got your name written all over it."

"What do you mean?"

"I mean exactly that. Your name is written on the shirt of the deceased, and I'm delivering the message."

Larkin listened to the details, hung up, and stood staring at the phone for a moment. "You'll have to excuse me, Mrs. Poe, Casey. I'll have somebody see to anything you might need. It'll just be a while. . . ."

A minute later he was at a wall map in an adjacent office, pointing things out to Ginny.

"The last transponder identification was here, northern Arizona. But the body lands here, in Fresno. And Lerner Airfield's in Death Valley." He pondered.

"Could they have turned around?"

"That's it! They turned around! They're coming back this way! Get me Devers."

She put in the call and handed him a headset.

He could hear the chopper noise. "Chief? Turn around, the plane's going to Lerner Airfield, a little strip in Death Valley!"

"Horseshit," Malloy broke in. "We're tailing their transponder tag into Arizona."

"Listen to me, you guys. A body fell out of the sky, in Fresno. It had a note on it!"

"We're right on their tail, Vince," Devers said. "Pilot says not more than thirty miles behind."

"Please, just listen. It was to me! The note on the body was to me!"

"Hold the details, Vince. We'll get back to you."

"Christ!" Larkin spat to the dead radio.

"No go?" Ginny said.

"I'm gone." He headed out the door, leaving her open-mouthed.

He found the transportation officer in a hangar. "I need a plane or a chopper."

"You and me both," the man said. "I'm all out."

"Nothing?"

"Nada."

"I got to get to Lerner Airfield, Death Valley, in forty minutes."

"Forty minutes? It's only about seventy miles. You could do it in a fast car, if you were Mario Andretti."

He dashed out, headed for his rusty Pinto in the parking lot. But on the way, something else caught his eye.

Duncan Malloy's hot Corvette sat there, beckoning to him. The key would be in the office.

Two minutes later he was wheeling out of the lot, and the last thing Ginny saw of him as she trotted out behind, trying to find out what was going on, was the vanity plate "AZZ KIKR" on the rear of the car.

He roared down the two-lane highway at speeds above 100, passing cars he hardly saw. Wearing Malloy's driving gloves and wraparound shades, he was busy on Malloy's cell phone.

"Troopers, Guard, whoever you got. Set up a secured perimeter two miles from the airfield and sit tight. Don't make contact until you hear from me."

An RV pulled out in front of him and he yanked the wheel too hard. The Corvette lost its grip on the road and spun, off to the shoulder, back onto the pavement, then twice more before coming to a rest half in a ditch.

"Whew!" Larkin said. He fired up again and took off. He had only twenty minutes left.

The leadership council was gathered in the cockpit.

"Don't they have a way of tracking these things?" Diamond Dog asked.

"They got radar," Swamp Thing said, "but that only goes so far."

"Then what?"

"What they call a transponder. Every aircraft's got one. Like a beeper, sends out a signal with your signature on it."

"Where's ours?"

"Gosh, Swamp," Cyrus said, feigning ignorance, "where's our transponder?"

"Well, less I miss my guess," Swamp Thing said, rubbing his big jaw, "the late Pinball deposited it in a little aircraft that right now oughta be not too far ahead of whatever's after it—somewhere around the Grand Canyon." He pointed to the empty space in the control panel.

Cindino chuckled. "A good job, well done."

The pilot leaned back toward Malloy and Devers. "We should be within a minute of visual contact, men."

They craned their necks to see.

Uncle Bob's sightseeing plane was over the

Grand Canyon's North Rim when suddenly the fleet of Huey and Cobra helicopters converged on him.

"What the fuck is that?" Malloy rasped.

"What the hell?" Devers said, squinting at the view. "We been bamboozled! That can't be the aircraft we're after. Call off the dogs! Get me Vince Larkin on the horn!"

TWELVE

Billy Bedlam foraged amid the convicts' banker's boxes in the freight compartment under the main fuselage floor. He was picking through them as if looking for a particular one—and not his own, for he put that one aside and kept looking.

Finally he found the one he wanted. The one with the happy face on it. The one marked "Poe." He opened it and smiled. He took out the bedraggled pink bunny and held it up for a look. He tossed it onto the floor. He found a letter in an official government envelope and opened it up. It was the letter announcing Cameron Poe's parole.

"Put the bunny back in the box," commanded Poe, coming out of the shadows behind him.

"I knew you weren't no lifer," Billy Bedlam proclaimed, waving the letter. "And lo and behold, you're a fucking parolee. You been turned on us the whole time, haven't you! You're a fucking rat, or the next thing closest to it! There's nothing lower than what you are."

"I said, put the bunny back in the box."

Billy Bedlam rose and took a step forward—planting his foot firmly on the pink bunny.

Poe's straight right sent him backward and made him spit out a tooth.

"Now I'm annoyed," Bedlam said, smiling. He charged at Poe headfirst, aiming to ram him in the belly.

But Poe's quick, sharp uppercut caught him flush on the jaw, straightened him, sent him reeling back.

He slammed backfirst into the jagged end of a strut, with such force that the strut went almost clear through. He would have been unconscious anyway, from the punch. Now he hung there dead.

"Why couldn't you just have put the bunny back in the box?" Poe said. He picked up the letter, folded it, and stuck it in his pocket where it was safer than in the box. He picked up the bunny, dusted it off, and laid it carefully in the box. He put the box back in the stack, with others on top of it, dusted off his hands, gave the area a quick scan—including the limp form of Billy Bedlam hanging like a side of beef—and walked back toward the hatch to the main cabin.

The C-123 was descending. Baby-O was dozing. Poe walked casually up the aisle from the hatch and sat down next to Garland Greene.

Greene smiled wryly at him. "Two went down the hatch. One came up." He waited for a response, but Poe was mum. "You don't have to tell me. I'm sure you had your reasons. He was a damaged boy, probably an abused child, almost certainly a hopeless prospect."

"He was a nut."

"Ah . . . the great ones—Dahmer, Gacy, Bundy—they were all nuts. Although I personally believe that sitting behind a desk for fifty years, then to be cast out like a sack of rotten oats with nothing to show for it, might be the most insane thing of all." He mused, looking at the ceiling. "For me, there've been so many. One girl—I drove through three states wearing her head as a hat."

"Feel free not to share everything with me." Poe got up and moved over to sit across the aisle to await the landing.

Cyrus the Virus sat down next to him. "This is some kind of situation we find ourselves in, isn't it?"

Poe didn't answer.

Cyrus looked past him, out the window. "When I heard they were building Feltham, I knew they would send me there. I'd be locked down twenty-four, seven. Every minute of every day. I also knew I'd never see it. I am no longer willing to live just for the privilege of breathing. Do you understand that?"

Poe looked at him. "Understand what?"

Cyrus sighed. "This has been years in the making, Cameron Poe, what you see going on here. And nothing will stop it."

"That a fact?"

"Prison tries to kill everything that's evil inside a man. Ends up killing everything, all the good, too."

"All your good dead, Cyrus?"

"Pretty much. I haven't had a good thought in years, Cameron Poe, not one. Until today."

"Today."

"Yes, today. Because today, one way or the other, we will be free."

"I'm not so interested in being free and dead, to be honest with you."

"That's what you think? Naw, we're better than that." He paused a while. "Tell me, Cameron Poe, what do you really want?"

Poe looked at him. "A cold beer."

"That's all?"

"Wife, daughter, grass, peace."

"Well, that's very nice." Cyrus leaned back and folded his hands in his lap and closed his eyes. "I must say, I'm not surprised you got a poetic bone in you, Cameron Poe. Brains, sense, sensitivity. Ah, yes. But those things we dream about, they're not going to happen. So let's get back to doing what we do so well—killing, maiming, making people miserable." He opened his eyes and smiled at Poe.

Poe leaned back and closed his eyes.

They descended through the low cloud ceiling, and a tiny landing strip for weekend aviators appeared below them, set in a belt of rugged, barren land, with the rectangles of a small trailer park nearby. A few hangars sat squat and gray against the brown ground, and here and there was a truck or other indistinguishable piece of equipment. One smaller hangar or storage building was covered not by a roof but by a tarpaulin. A small control tower rose like a mushroom. An old airplane boneyard looked like a scattering of broken toys.

Off to the left a ways, an insignificant little blot on the clear desert sky, a single-engine Cessna also approached the small field.

Swamp Thing spoke over the intercom. "All right, you moldy peckerwoods, wipe the drool off your chins and zip up your pantaloons—we're about to touch down."

Larkin took a couple of deep breaths before he got out of the Corvette, and even then his legs were shaky for a few minutes after the hairy drive.

He had parked in a small storage shed where the car was more or less out of sight. Cautiously he approached the small control tower, went in, and soundlessly climbed the stairs.

He heard a radio, a communication from a pilot: "Hey, Lerner tower, what gives? Cessna 4737. I need a response. Screw it, I'm coming in anyway."

He entered the control room, looking carefully around. It was empty, deserted. "Anybody home?"

There was a rumpled copy of *Penthouse* on the console. On the magazine were some dark drops, still wet. He dabbed his index finger in a drop and smelled it. It was blood.

He drew his gun from the holster in the middle of his lower back. There was one closet. He stepped to it, paused, then yanked the door open.

A man in a white shirt lay crumpled on the floor, earphones cocked on his head and his throat cut.

Larkin shut the door. There was a pleasant buzz outside, and through the window he saw the Cessna land. Then there was a roar that caused him to drop to the floor. The C-123 made a pass so close he thought it would blow in the windows.

He crawled over to the console and grabbed the radio mike, but the cord had been severed.

All in all, he deduced, this was not a good place to be. He ran out and down the stairs and headed for the shed.

. . .

Swamp Thing completed his low pass, hee-hawing the whole way, and banked into his final approach for landing. He lowered the landing gear. He saw the Cessna on the runway, taxiing slowly.

"Better move aside, potlicker, 'cause I'm coming in! Haw!" Swamp Thing grinned and lowered the nose of the Provider.

The pilot of the Cessna saw the C-123 on a collision course at the last second he had, and he swerved to the left and skidded off the runway into the dirt just as the C-123 wingtip whooshed by.

"Yeee-haaaw!" howled Swamp Thing as the tires of the Provider screeched in contact with the asphalt. In winning his game of chicken with the Cessna, he had come in too fast. He reversed pitch of the props, and the engines whined. He hit the brakes, and the tail swished back and forth.

"Hold on!" yelled Swamp Thing as the C-123 smashed through a line of crash barrels at the end of the runway, exploded a wooden fence, slid across a dirt road, and headed for a twenty-foot-long propane tank. It slowed, slowed, and finally was jarred to a stop a few feet from the propane by a pond of mud into which the nosewheel sank.

Throughout the plane there were exhalations of relief, sighs, low moans. Diamond Dog opened the cages, releasing the guards.

But as Bishop started out, Cyrus the Virus

stepped in front and put up a hand. "Not so fast. We don't need any distractions. Lock her back up." He pushed her into the cage and Diamond Dog closed the lock.

They started to file out of the mired plane. Larkin watched from inside the storage shed, through the spaces between the wall slats.

"Lerner Airfield," Cyrus said. "Never been more glad to be someplace. So . . ." he looked slowly around, "where's the plane, Francisco?"

Cindino paced nervously back and forth. "Don't worry about it. Don't worry about it. Have patience."

Cyrus stepped in front of him and put his face close. "Patience, my friend? Last guy that told me to have patience, I burned him down and bagged his ashes."

"Please," Cindino scoffed, waving him away, "don't offend me with crude anecdotes. Cyrus, my friend, it will be here."

The pilot of the Cessna appeared from around the tail of the C-123, his jaw set in anger. "Hey! What the hell do you boys think you're . . . Jesus!" He gaped at the cons emerging from the plane and gathering around him. "Never mind, never mind . . . it's . . . nothing. . . ."

He turned and ran off the field and into the desert, never looking back.

"Hope he likes salt," Cyrus said. "Johnny," he said to Johnny Twenty-Three, "get up on that tower and have a look-see. Let's go get us some firepower." He turned to Cindino. "You come with me."

Johnny Twenty-Three jogged toward the tower, which was amid the hangars and sheds and equipment a hundred yards away. Garland Greene wandered off in the other direction.

Swamp Thing debarked and went around to check the nosewheel.

Sally Can't Dance passed by. "Very glamorous. This place is perfect for me. Nice landing, by the way. Very smooth."

"Up yours, doofus."

"Don't mind if I do." Sally sashayed away.

On the plane, Poe attempted to lift Baby-O. "Come on, bro, we're getting off."

"Oh, man, Poe, I don't think I can make it. I don't think I can even stand up."

"I don't think you should move him," said Bishop, watching from the cage. "He's too far along, could go into anaphylactic shock."

"She's right, bro," Baby-O said. "You go."

"Not without you."

Baby-O laughed weakly. "Here we go, Ranger boy. Got to be a hero, no such thing as leaving a fallen comrade, right? Get real, bro. Get outta here."

"He's right," Bishop said. "Best you just leave."

Poe thought a moment. "Okay, here's how it goes. I'm gonna find a needle—got to be a first-aid kit around somewhere out there. And I'll come back and fix you. Then we'll crawl stylishly out of here."

"Do what you gotta do, bro." Baby-O closed his eyes.

"Just don't crap out on me."

They tapped fists.

Poe walked past Bishop. "I'll be back for you, too," he said quietly.

"Later," she said.

Poe walked down the rear ramp and around to the side of the plane. He stopped. In front of him he saw six guards on their knees, looking up into the barrel of a pistol being leveled at them by Diamond Dog.

"What the hell you doing?" Poe barked.

"What's it look like?" Diamond Dog said. "We gotta put 'em down."

"You can't do that, Dog."

"Tell me why, soldier. Make it convincing. 'Cause I been waiting a long time for this particular opportunity—eleventeen years or something like that."

"They're hostages," Poe said. "We need them."

Diamond Dog slowly turned and aimed the gun

at Poe's head, smiling slightly. "And just what's it to you, soldier?"

"I want all the protection I can get," Poe said, "in order to get out of here. They're protection."

Diamond Dog narrowed his eyes. "I don't understand you. I watch you. But I don't understand you. Who are you?"

Poe studied him. Dog was sweating, maybe he was losing it a bit. But Poe didn't dare misjudge him. Diamond Dog would shoot him for sure, if he felt like it.

"What you say, white man?" Dog went on. "Any answer?"

"White man is fine. Just a white man trying not to die."

"Nothing's ever just black and white. But from where I'm standing, it should be all black."

"Nothing's ever all black either, pal. Putting those men down ain't gonna change their color. Putting me down ain't gonna change yours."

"You like those guys?"

"Shit, man, up to me, I'd put a bullet in the brain of every one. But there's other folks dependent on us for good decisions." He spat in the direction of the guards. "My question is, how well do you know this Cindino? I read somewhere he firebombed that prime minister's yacht, with two of his own cousins on board."

Diamond Dog pursed his lips. "What's your point?"

"Man kills his own cousins, probably wouldn't think twice about dropping some hired guns once they'd served his purpose."

"You think he sees us as hired guns?"

"What do you think?"

"Shit. . . ."

Cyrus strode up to the group, looked at the guards, then at Poe and Dog. "What exactly is going on here?"

"Giantkiller didn't want me to drop these bulls," Dog said, his eyes never leaving Poe.

"Really?" Cyrus looked at Poe.

"Really," Dog said.

Cyrus looked Poe up and down. "Now, I can understand why Nathan here wants to kill the guards. What I don't get is, why don't you, Cameron Poe?"

Poe was silent for a time. "Cyrus, this is your barbecue. You're gonna do it your way. If it was my play, I'd wait for that bird to get airborne before I start eliminating our only leverage." He shrugged. "Just that I think it's sloppy work, knocking them down for no reason that relates to the operation. That kind of stuff ain't professional. Gets in the way. But shit, I'm in either way, you know that."

"Fuck this." Diamond Dog stalked over and put the gun to the first guard in the row.

"Put the heat down, Nathan," Cyrus said, firmly.

"Oh, man. . . ."

"Things have changed." He looked off to where Cindino was pacing. "We go to Plan B. We need a refueling truck and a tractor. We need the hostages."

It was brutally hot in the shed, probably hotter even than out on the asphalt, because the sun beat down on the roof and baked the innards.

Larkin felt a knot in the pit of his stomach as he watched the tableau. He was at first sure that all the guards kneeling in the dirt near the mudhole were going to be executed. Then it looked like a bluff. Then he saw the pistol again placed at the head of one of the guards, and lowered. He couldn't tell who was calling the shots. The big black guy with the shaved head and the tattoo on his neck, whom he remembered as Nathan "Diamond Dog" Jones, was the initial executioner. Then along came the other guy with the shaved head who smiled a lot, Cyrus "the Virus" Grissom. Cons seemed to defer to him. Then there was that guy Poe. Larkin's reading of him was crucial. Did he have any power here?

Could he be sure of his assumptions about Cameron Poe? What if he was wrong? And if he was right, that Poe was in fact an ally of his in this situation, would Poe survive it?

He crept around the shed for a better view.

"Wonder where Cindino's plane is," Cyrus said, scratching his bald head. "We gotta get out of here pretty quick."

"What if there ain't no plane?" Poe said. "Just a thought." It would be better, Poe thought, if he could get them to stick with this C-123, slow and recognizable—and just now stuck in the mud.

Cyrus walked around the buried nosewheel, where Swamp Thing was scratching his head. "Okay, boys, let's dig."

From the stash of tools in a hangar, they found shovels and began digging around the wheel.

"My daddy taught me that many hands make light work," Cyrus said. "What'd your daddy teach you, Cameron Poe?"

"My daddy?" Poe chuckled. "To look out."

Cyrus laughed. "You got a good education, then. Man, it's hot. Yo, Viking!" Cyrus summoned a tall blond con with a ponytail. Viking was a farm boy of few words and few actions, but a strong back and good hands. "About time to get a tractor."

"Where?"

Poe tossed his shovel aside. "I'll go get the fuel truck."

"I say, Cameron Poe," Cyrus said, smiling, "you are a most useful human being."

"Cindino!"

Francisco Cindino, looking around the airfield nervously, ceased his pacing to and fro and came over.

"Here." Cyrus held out a shovel.

"You're not serious."

"Dig, man, like your life depended on it."

THIRTEEN

Garland Greene counted twenty-one trailers in the park. Almost all were decrepit, some appeared to be vacant. Ahead of him was an empty swimming pool, its walls cracked and crumbling. He walked casually ahead. He heard a soft, tinkling voice—like a fairy, he thought.

On the concrete floor of the shallow end of the pool, a little girl, maybe five, played with dolls. She looked up and smiled.

"Hi," Greene said.

"What's your name?"

"Garland."

She wrinkled her nose. "Garland. That's a funny name."

"What's your name?"

"Susan."

"That's a nice name. Can I play with you?"

"You can play with me. Come down that ladder over there."

Poe and Viking walked past the hangars. They found a tractor first, in the shadow of a hangar, an old red Farmall with a rusty seat. Viking climbed onto it. Up on that perch he looked around and pointed toward the small, low building covered by a tarpaulin. "Fuel truck," he said.

Poe headed for the depot where Viking had spotted the truck. He glanced back and noticed that Cindino, holding a shovel, was following him with his eyes.

The fuel truck was half hidden behind the storage depot, the cab visible to the C-123, but not the tank. Poe got to the truck, climbed in, and started the engine. But he didn't drive it out. Instead he got out and went to the rear, unclamped the hose and unreeled it from its spool, put the nozzle on the ground on a slight incline toward a ditch, pulled the lever, and watched the precious fuel spill onto the ground and gurgle away.

He looked around to make sure he couldn't be seen from the plane, edged over to the depot, raised the tarpaulin flap, and went in.

In the dim, dusty light he saw a desk and some

boxes piled up. Behind them, separating this area from the main part of the depot, was a broad curtain.

He knelt down to open the lid of a crate. Everything went black.

The man in a safari jacket had slugged Poe at the base of the skull with the butt of a handgun, and now he and his cohort dragged him across the floor, through an opening in the curtain, to where a sleek green-and-white Learjet stood like a predator about to jump.

The Farmall, dragging a length of cable, chugged along toward the Provider, Viking occasionally looking back, expecting to see the fuel truck behind him. The tractor bucked to a stop beside the plane.

"Where's the fuel truck at?" Swamp Thing said, picking up the end of the cable and walking it around to the tail hook.

The men continued to dig, the wheel was almost free. Cindino climbed out of the hole, glancing over at the storage depot.

"Where indeed?" Cyrus said, scanning the field.

Viking shrugged.

Across the road came the hulking Conrad, his Mohawk haircut glistening in the sun, pushing a shopping cart laden with goods. "Check it out!" he sang, pointing to bottles of liquor, a boom-box radio, magazines, cans of food.

"Not bad," Cyrus said, taking a box of cheroots out of the cart. "Where from?"

"Some kinda little store," Conrad said, waving back where he had come from. "The old guy in there scrammed right away when I jumped over the counter."

Cyrus lit the cigar and continued to scan the area, looking for the fuel truck.

Garland Greene sat on the concrete with the little girl, holding the boy doll while she held the girl doll.

" 'It's nice to see you, John,' " she said, bobbing the head of her doll up and down in the rhythm of speech. " 'Would you like to come over for dinner?' Now you have to make John talk."

" 'I'd love to come for dinner, Jan,' " Garland said, making his doll's head bob.

" 'That's fine. We'll be having burgers and beans.' " She looked up. "Did you come in that big plane?" She watched Garland nod. "It woke me up. Are you sick?"

"What makes you think that?"

"Your face is very pale. When I'm sick, Mommy says my face is pale."

"I'm sick."

"Do you take medicine?"

Garland paused. "There is no medicine for my sickness." He squirmed around.

She made her doll dance. "You want to sing?"

"Sing what?"

"Can we sing 'He's Got the Whole World in His Hands'?"

"I may not remember all the words."

"I'll teach you. Come on. . . ."

They began to sing.

Poe sat on the floor, his hands on top of his head, looking up at the two men standing in front of him, one holding a handgun. A black Glock automatic. His head ached, and he was dizzy. He struggled to focus and clear his head and sort it out, to take in everything, be sure what he should say and what he shouldn't.

"Cindino's plane," he said. "Already here." He looked from one face to the other, searching for reactions, however minor. They were stony. "So you're going to take Cindino and ditch everybody else." He didn't know how far he should push them, trying to make them react, give up some information.

The men didn't look at each other, just kept their languid eyes on Poe.

"So now you gotta deal with me."

The man on the right raised the gun and sighted at Poe's head.

"You won't shoot," Poe said evenly, "because you know that twenty convicts will hear you. So you've gotta do something else."

The man on the left smiled. The man with the gun reached into the pocket of his safari jacket and pulled out a six-inch silencer and screwed it onto the barrel of the gun.

"I see," Poe said. "But what's the point? I'm no threat. You're not gonna kill everybody."

"Dee point ees," the man on the left said, still smiling, "we don't wanna worry 'bout you, meester."

The other man put the silenced barrel against Poe's temple. Poe kept his eyes open and staring at the other man.

"Freeze!"

The men spun to see Larkin step through the curtain, face stained with sweat, holding his pistol in both hands at arm's length.

He took sideways steps behind the men. "Just freeze!"

Poe sprang to his feet, smashed his elbow into the face of the man with the silenced gun, his toe into the belly of the other, then slugged each in turn with left-right combinations as they went down.

They lay unconscious, sprawled on the concrete. Poe quickly stepped over their outstretched arms and retrieved the Glock. He straightened up to aim the gun at Larkin, just as Larkin's gun was now trained on him.

"Now what?" Poe said, since Larkin hadn't pulled the trigger when he just as well could have.

"You're Cameron Poe."

Poe didn't answer.

"I'm Larkin."

"Hello, Larkin."

"You sent me that message, on the body."

"You got troops?"

"They'll be here," Larkin said. "Can I put my firearm away?"

"Go ahead."

"You'll put yours down?"

Poe was silent.

"You don't trust me. But look, Poe. I thought I could help you get off that plane, keep the plane on the ground, keep people alive."

Poe remained silent, they both held the guns steady.

"What's this aircraft here?" Larkin said.

"Francisco Cindino's buggy. He was their way out."

"He's a drug lord, son of the biggest."

"Looks like he was running a scam on everybody," said Poe. "Where's the pilot?"

"Pilot?"

"I don't think these guys are pilots. Cindino isn't either. Somebody's gotta be around to fly this plane."

"We'll find him," Larkin said.

Poe wagged his head slightly toward the Learjet.

Larkin nodded, without looking at the jet. "Okay. We gotta think this through, make a plan."

"I'm going back to the C-123."

"Why? Poe, you're a free man, if you don't get screwed up with all this. I'm not tying you into it, not yet, not if you don't do anything stupid. You're still clean, far as I know. Help me now."

"I got friends on board." Poe started edging for the curtain.

"I talked to your wife. In my office. And your little girl."

Poe stopped. "You saw Tricia and Casey?"

"They can't wait to see you."

Poe chewed his lip. "Tell them I love them. Tell them I couldn't leave my guys behind. They'll understand. Leave a light on. I'll get back."

"You're not gonna help me?"

"Marshal Larkin, I been helping you all along. Trust me. Later." He slid out the curtain.

Larkin waited a couple of minutes, then dragged Cindino's unconscious men one by one out through the curtain.

Poe didn't go directly back to the Provider but found the tiny store behind the airfield's gas station, which Conrad had visited a few minutes before and virtually emptied of stock. But Poe wasn't looking for goods to eat and drink. He rummaged through cabinets frantically, throwing things aside until he found a small emergency safety kit. He popped it open and sifted through the contents: Band-Aids, cotton, Mercurochrome, tape.

"Damn!" There was nothing for Baby-O. His buddy was in a critical state. No point in going back to the plane without being able to help Baby-O. The irony was, had they remained in prison, they would have had whatever they needed. Now, out here where there was no law or confinement at all, he was helpless to help Baby-O.

Johnny Twenty-Three stood atop the control tower and scanned the horizon. Then he began to hop up and down. He ripped off his shirt and waved it. "Yo! Cons!" he yelled. "We got company!"

Cyrus looked at Johnny, then looked away in the direction he was pointing. A few miles away, coming down a long tongue of road and trailing rooster tails of dust, was a convoy of vehicles, heading their way.

"My, my, my," Cyrus said. He stomped over to where a cable from the tractor was attached to the tail hook of the C-123, and the men were finishing their digging. "Step it up, boys. I think we got a rat among us. I wonder who the rat is." He stepped up to the tractor. "Viking, how far away are they?"

Viking rubbed his chin as he looked off toward the convoy. "Seven miles."

"So that's ten, twelve minutes at the most," Diamond Dog said.

"Haul that plane outta there!" Cyrus ordered.

Viking fired up the Farmall. He moved forward until the cable was taut. Then he shoved the throttle forward. The engine roared, the nose of the tractor reared up. He throttled back and signaled for other cons to sit on the axle to hold the front down. Then he fired up again. The Provider edged backward slowly out of the ooze and up out of the mudhole and onto the road.

"Where's Cindino?" Cyrus said, looking around. "Where the fuck's Cindino?"

"He was digging," Diamond Dog said. "Then he left."

"Left where?"

"Just walked out of the hole, that's all I saw."

Francisco Cindino slunk across the airfield, then broke into a run, slipped under the flap of the tarpaulin, and bolted up the stairs into the Learjet. "*Vamonos! Vamonos!*" he yelled, charging toward the cockpit, where the pilot was cowering on the floor. "Let's get the hell out of here, *idiota!*"

The pilot, his white shirt drenched with sweat, scrambled up into his seat and leaned to the control panel to fire up the engines.

Larkin, who had seen Cindino dash by, now heard the initial whine of the twin jets just before the blast from them flipped up the curtain and knocked him out through the tarpaulin wall.

The jet's nose burst through the front tarpaulin, and the plane headed for the runway, escorted by the wide-eyed, drop-jawed looks from the convicts assembled in stunned silence around the Provider. When Cyrus's mouth fell open, he almost dropped his cigar.

Unseen by the convicts watching the Learjet, Larkin sprinted along, parallel to the jet, behind stacks of oil barrels and gas pumps, toward a yellow construction crane. He leaped aboard, slid into the driver's seat, scanned the levers, put his hand on one, and looked out to see the Learjet coming alongside almost abreast of him, starting its takeoff run. At that instant, he pulled the hydraulics lever, releasing the crane boom, which fell like a guillotine.

The boom fell on the jet's fuselage near the rear, slicing through the thin aluminum shell. The front of the jet, separated from the rear, spun and slid in a path that brought it smack into the gas pumps. The broken pumps spewed gasoline over the severed jet nose in which Cindino and his pilot struggled to free themselves from their harnesses.

Cyrus took a puff on his cigar. "Stay here!" he commanded the rest of the cons. "Get this plane ready to roll! Come on, Dog!"

He and Diamond Dog ran for the front piece of the Learjet.

Cindino got out of his harness first, tried his door, and found it jammed from the collision. He whacked the window three times before it gave and popped out in pieces.

He stuck his head through to see Cyrus and Diamond Dog staring up at him. He pulled his head back in and slumped in his seat.

Diamond Dog went over to see who had been operating the crane, but found the cab empty.

Larkin had jumped out and sprinted away toward a rusty old International dump truck that had a snowplow mounted on the front.

Cyrus called up to the cockpit: "Hey, Francisco! Looks like you and me had different ideas about this getaway."

Cindino's head popped out again. "I can explain."

"Oh, I understand, Francisco." He took three quick puffs on his cigar. "Wish I could hang around to chat. Wish your jet was still together, because we sure could use it. But, hey," he shrugged, "we'll miss you, too."

Cyrus flicked the glowing cigar into the pool of gasoline and walked quickly away. The flames raced around the jet and under it. The plane went up in a fireball that blew out what was left of the gas station.

Cameron Poe, having just left the store, was knocked down by the blast, the pistol sent skittering away in a direction he didn't see. He rolled under the hulk of an old truck and found himself beside a trembling elderly man—the man Conrad had frightened off on his earlier visit to the store.

"Don't kill me," the man pleaded.

"I need a syringe," Poe said.

"Wh . . . what's a syringe?"

"For giving shots, like a doctor."

"Don't kill me, don't give me a shot."

"There's gotta be some first-aid stuff around here."

"Over there, maybe." He pointed along the ground. "Behind the propane tanks, there's a case with a red cross on it."

Poe tapped his hand. "Thanks. Stay here. You'll be safe."

He rolled out and crept toward the pile of small propane tanks near the big ones where the Provider had been stuck in the mud.

Swamp Thing had a couple of wrenches and was working on the front wheel.

Cyrus bent over, hands on knees, to check the situation. "What's up? We gotta load up, close the ramp, and get out of here."

"Brakes."

"How long before she's ready to fly?"

"I need ten minutes."

"Too long. We got the cavalry coming." Now in the narrowing distance Cyrus could see markings of Army, National Guard, police, on the vehicles churning toward the airfield.

"I saw the column. So what you want from me? This wheel won't roll for takeoff until I get it loose."

"Well, that's a problem."

"Leave me alone, you ain't helping none."

A nearby gunshot attracted Cyrus's attention, and then, "Hey, Cyrus, look here."

Diamond Dog had blasted the lock on the belly cargo compartment of the plane and found the small arsenal of shotguns, pistols, tear-gas canisters, and boxes of ammo.

Cyrus walked over. "Wow!"

"No, no, that ain't it. I mean, yeah, we got guns. But looked up inside."

Cyrus squatted down and looked up inside. He saw the body of Billy Bedlam hanging on the point of the strut. He frowned.

"Whatcha think?" Diamond Dog asked.

"The plot thickens." He stood up. "But we ain't got time for mysteries right now." He looked around. "Conrad! You keep an eye on the guards. Everybody else!" He waved at the group. "Grab the guns, grab those propane tanks, grab everything! Over to the boneyard!" He waved to the area of old retired and cannibalized planes to the rear of the C-123. "We'll take positions around those old planes. Ambush, boys! Let's give that convoy everything we've got!"

Everybody but Swamp Thing rallied at the arms supply. Swamp Thing continued to work on the plane's brakes.

Guns and ammo and canisters were quickly snatched up. Four of the cons took armloads of

propane tanks and laid them down around the
boneyard and opened the valves; gas hissed out,
heavier than air, spreading over the ground.

Johnny Twenty-Three, though, slid away from
the rest and crept up the ramp into the cabin of the
C-123. He saw Baby-O shivering in his seat. He
saw Bishop in her cage, and that made him smile.

He tried the door of the cage, found it locked.

"Forget it, Johnny," Bishop said. "I can't come
out to play."

He scouted around, and in the tool bay found a
crowbar. He began prying at the lock as Bishop
retreated to the rear of the cage.

"Don't do it, man," Baby-O said in a quavering
voice, unable to move from his seat. "Please don't
do it."

"Sorry, Baby-O, but you can't stop love."

The government vehicles had arrived in the area,
and the lawmen fanned out to approach the airfield, some of them cautiously approaching the
C-123, others creeping through the boneyard.

The ambush was skillfully set up; clearly none of
the advancing troops had a clue of what awaited
them. All around them, convicts had guns trained
on them, waiting for the right moment. Diamond

Dog held a tear-gas gun. Cyrus had all the convicts watching his raised hand for the signal.

The lead lawmen stopped and sniffed. "Gas!" one of them yelled. Immediately, the whole group turned and began to run back the way they'd come.

"Now!" Cyrus lowered his hand.

Diamond Dog fired a tear-gas round into the propane mist, and one by one the tanks exploded into the air. Simultaneously, the convicts opened fire on the retreating lawmen. Cops and soldiers fell, others dove for cover and started firing back—for the most part blindly in the beginning, until they began to get a fix on where the opposing fire was coming from. Two more lawmen slumped over, but now convicts began to take hits, too.

Cyrus saw that Swamp Thing had freed the Provider from the cable, indicating the plane was ready to go. "Back to the plane!" he hollered, waving to the cons. "Back to the plane! Let's go!"

FOURTEEN

Cameron Poe found the case with the red cross on it, and a sign that said, "Medical Personnel Only!" He smashed the lock with a shovel and scanned the supplies. This was a more serious cache of medical gear. He opened several cases until he found one with two syringes and some tiny bottles of fluid.

Just then the firing broke out. He grabbed a syringe and two bottles of fluid and ran out.

But what he was about to run into was a crossfire between the convicts and lawmen, and between him and the open rear ramp of the C-123. He stopped and assessed the action, saw he had no choice, and tucked his head down to run the gauntlet of gunfire and get to the plane with his precious implements.

He dashed for the rear ramp, aware, as bullets

spattered around him, that Swamp Thing was already releasing the cable; the bird was ready to fly. Swamp Thing disappeared into the plane.

But that wasn't the only problem awaiting him.

Inside, Johnny had managed to crowbar the lock, and was now stepping into the cage. Bishop kicked at him and swung rights and lefts ineffectively.

"Just the way I like 'em," he said, "hot and active." He grabbed her, forced her into a choke hold, and tightened his grip until she began to sag. Then he dragged her down.

Poe made it to the plane and started up the ramp when he saw the cable lying on the ground. He jumped off the ramp and grabbed the near end and attached it back to the tail of the plane, then he took the loose end and ran with it twenty yards to a cement pylon, where he slipped the cable hook into the eyebolt in the top of the pylon. He turned back for the rear ramp and saw that the cons were retreating from the boneyard, firing as they came.

Johnny clawed at Bishop's pants. Suddenly his head was yanked back. Poe had him by the hair. For an instant, Johnny could look up into Poe's eyes. Then his face was smashed down on the floor, again and again, until things went blank.

Poe flung Johnny to the side of the cage and

cradled Bishop's head. Normal color was returning to her face, and her eyes flicked open.

"You okay?" Poe asked.

"Getting there. Take care of your buddy. He's bad."

Poe ducked out of the cage and across the aisle to Baby-O. He uncapped the syringe, stuck it in the fluid, drew some in, and took Baby-O's arm.

Baby-O's eyes fluttered open. "Hey, bro," he said weakly. "Whatcha got?"

"Fixin's, bro. You're gonna be all right."

"Oh, man, you got saint's blood. I'll do it. Gimme that. I got more experience than you. You got bad guys coming in. You got more experience with that."

Poe handed him the syringe. "Do it and let's go."

Baby-O fumbled with the syringe, trying to get his fingers to work.

The plane shook as the engines started. Swamp Thing urged the Provider into a slow taxi forward.

Cyrus led his men back to the plane—only about half of them were left. "Go, go, go!" He waved them toward the yawning rear ramp.

Diamond Dog hung back, providing covering fire, and as he glanced behind him toward the plane, he saw the cable slithering along the ground, tightening. "What the fuck?"

Then he saw that it was connected to the pylon. He dropped his shotgun and ran.

Inside the plane, Poe could see that Dog had discovered the attachment to the pylon and was heading for it. "Come on, come on!" he pleaded to Baby-O.

Baby-O had succeeded in getting the needle into his arm, and anticipated the relief. "Aaaah," he crooned, slumping back in his seat.

Diamond Dog lunged for the hook and slipped it free from the pylon, tumbling into a complete somersault from the effort, and he scrambled on all fours to regain his footing and get to the plane while bullets stitched the ground around him.

"Let's go, bro!" Poe said. "This buzzard's gonna leave!"

"I just gotta breathe—"

"Now!" Poe pulled Baby-O to his feet and started to half drag him toward the rear hatch, Bishop coming behind them.

Over the sound of the gunfire came another sound: helicopters, Hueys and Cobras, were joining the action, churning the air overhead. And yet another sound: The old dump truck with the snowplow was crashing through the boneyard, flipping airplane carcasses and pieces aside.

Larkin raised the plow halfway, using it as a shield against the bullets. He charged ahead through the boneyard and up the road beside the runway, parallel to the path of the plane as it began its takeoff run.

"Come on, come on, you old bastard!" Larkin pounded on the wheel as if he could whip it into more speed like a horse, as he tried to keep pace with the plane.

From the tail hook, the cable, now released from the pylon, writhed and slashed like a desperate snake, slapping lethally at anything within twenty yards of the plane.

Faster, faster the plane moved, edging ahead of Larkin's dump truck, which was now nearly shaking apart from the vibration of the old engine trying to impel the old parts. "Don't lose it, you old bastard!" Larkin said, through gritted teeth.

He didn't know what he would do if he could get ahead of the plane—just that he had to get there and stop it somehow. At first he had thought he could just bump it over with the plow, like forcing a car off the road. Now it looked more and more as though he'd never get close enough even to touch the machine; and just for now he hated the efficiency of the blue-and-white aircraft that his own agency had maintained all too well.

In front of him, the wild cable swung and slashed. He could see it would whip into the wooden shed where he had hidden Malloy's Corvette.

In a split second, the cable did just that, and more. It sliced through the wooden wall and instantly whacked into the Corvette, and, too fast for Larkin's eye to capture it, the cable wrapped itself three times around the chrome bumper and snapped tight.

The Corvette was ripped through the shed, exploding a hail of wood, and was yanked into position behind the C-123 and hauled wildly down the runway.

Larkin braked to a stop, awed by the event, and got out.

Swamp Thing pulled back on the control column, and the nose of the C-123 jerked into the air. The plane left the runway and began its climb. The Corvette swung airborne behind it.

Poe and Baby-O and Bishop made it to the half-closed rear hatch in time to see that they were a hundred feet off the ground.

In the air off to the side, another hundred feet up, the Army Huey carrying Devers and Malloy hovered over the action. They were as open-mouthed at what they saw as the convicts had been when the Learjet burst through the tarpaulin.

What they saw was the C-123 Provider taking off and dangling a load like a deep-sea fisherman hauling in a tarpon.

"Good lord, Duncan," Devers said, pointing a shaking finger at the sight. "Isn't that your car?"

Malloy's jaw kept opening and closing, like a tarpon out of water, and he looked fish-eyed to boot.

The Provider was unstable, its rear ramp refusing to close all the way, its tail drooping and slewing from the added weight, and it was forced into an unending steep bank to port in order to keep from plummeting back to earth.

In the cockpit of the cargo plane, Swamp Thing was fighting the controls in ways he knew he shouldn't. He knew that you felt your machine, talked to it through your hands, sensed what it needed, where it wanted to go, and you didn't so much force it to go against its will as cajole it to respond to you.

"What the fuck is wrong with this buzzard!" he hollered to no one in particular. "We got revs, we got manifold pressure, we got power, we oughta have five thousand horses. But we ain't goin' nowhere. It's like we're still stuck in the mud down there. *What the fuck is hanging us up?*"

Diamond Dog hopped into the cockpit. "We're pulling a car, Thing. We got hooked onto a damn *car!*"

Swamp Thing craned his neck to look as far back and below as he could, and there it was. "Fuckin' *Mustang!*" he spat. "We'll see about that!"

"Corvette, Thing. It's a Corvette."

"Hold on," Swamp Thing said. He maneuvered

the latest tight circle into a slight adjustment, and on the next pass the Corvette hit the control tower, snapping off the cable, and the car dropped to earth.

The C-123, free of its burden, now climbed steadily up and away, in odd profile because of the half-open rear ramp, and it soon vanished in the mountain cloud under the high Nevada sky.

Malloy's Corvette landed upside down and sent up a cloud of dust so furious and thick that nobody could see what had happened for a full fifteen seconds.

One of the first to witness the result was the little girl, Susan, who stood at the edge of the trailer park, waving at the disappearing cargo plane. "Good-bye, Garland. Come again soon."

She heard the crash, saw the cloud of dust, watched it dissipate, and went running home. "Mommy, Mommy, a flat pile of junk just fell out of the sky!"

The pilot set the Huey down, along with the other helicopters, and Malloy sprang out.

Larkin ran past him.

"Where do you think you're going?" Malloy cried.

"I'm gonna get that plane down, my way."

"Bullshit. You're not going anywhere."

Larkin jumped into the first Cobra, in the gunner's seat in front of the pilot. "Let's go!" he commanded, goosing the air with his thumb and pulling the helmet on.

"They call me Gator," the pilot said in the intercom. "Where to?"

"Find the contrails, Gator. We're still after that C-123."

Inside the C-123, the scene and mood were grim. Several convicts were wounded, some of those were dying. The floor was slippery with blood. Groans and moans from the convicts, and a whistling of the wind from the half-open rear hatch, made the atmosphere eerie.

Poe looked over at Bishop, chained again outside a cage. "How you doing?"

"Breathing, Poe. That's a start."

He rubbed Baby-O's head. "How you feeling, bro?"

Baby-O stretched luxuriously. "No pain, bro. Better and better. I'm a new man."

Swamp Thing sat hunched over the controls in a dark mood, his lips in a pout.

" 'Sup, Thing?" Diamond Dog said. "You ain't your normal escaped-felon self."

"We lost one of the Pratt & Whitneys back there."

Diamond Dog wrinkled his nose. "What does that mean, exactly?"

"It means," Cyrus the Virus put in, "we lost one engine, we better not lose another. We only had two this morning."

Diamond Dog looked out at one wing, then the other. "What I don't understand is, it looks like we still got the two."

"Jesus, Dog," Swamp Thing said, exasperated, "it means one don't work! It didn't evaporate completely."

"Oh. How come?"

"We put it under a lot of strain with that stuff back there. We could haul a car inside, easy. But with that sucker swingin' around underneath us like a damn yo-yo, that'll bugger things up. We got shook up pretty good back there."

Cyrus put a hand on Diamond Dog's shoulder. "Dog, go down under and make sure we ain't got damage or anything rolling around loose in the cargo compartment."

"Me?"

"You been there before, you can see if anything's been shook around."

"Aaw. . . ."

"We ain't gonna make good time, Cyrus," Swamp Thing growled. "Get used to that idea."

"Well, we do what we can. Meanwhile, I got a varmint to sniff out."

"What's a varmint?" Diamond Dog said.

"There's a rodent among us, Dog. Scat."

Diamond Dog headed for the hatch to the cargo compartment under the cabin floor.

Some of the convicts were doing their best to lighten the mood, or at least enjoy themselves while they could in a crippled cargo plane at 10,000 feet fleeing a posse of federal gunmen determined to lock them up forever or send them down in flames.

Sally Can't Dance, dressed now in a frilly cocktail-waitress uniform she found somewhere near the airfield, and Conrad, flush with expectations from his supply of store-stolen goods, passed out booze and chips and cigarettes. Soon the main cabin was filled with butt smoke and alcohol breath and loud jokes, to go with the moans and blood of wounded men and the dirt and sweat of everybody who had dug the plane out and dodged the government bullets.

Cyrus stepped into the cabin from the cockpit and looked around before he started down the aisle. When he came to the first cage, he looked in on Johnny Twenty-Three, whom Bishop had managed to manacle to the inside of the cage wall earlier with her own cuffs when he was sleeping off the effects of Cameron Poe's pounding.

Cyrus shook his head and clucked. "You know, you hate to see that, a perfectly good young rapist with excellent credentials humiliated by a locked-up broad in plain sight of some of the meanest men in the Western world."

"Come on, man," Johnny moaned, "get me out."

"But you know, some people are just born to lose." Cyrus walked on, giving an unwelcomed wink to Bishop who was now handcuffed to the second cage.

Conrad took his elbow. "Cyrus, I can understand taking Cindino out like that, with what he was trying to pull. But now what? Without him and his jet, what do we do?"

Cyrus faced the cabin. "Listen up, everybody!"

They gathered around.

"Okay, boys. What we do now is called plan B. Plan B is a strip in La Cartoza, Mexico. This cozy little area is inhabited by some heroin-dealer friends of mine. You don't need any more details at this time. But I'll tell you this about that: The wine runs like water, and the women nip at your heels like new pups."

The convicts yelled their approval, exchanged nods and smiles and hopeful words. Even the wounded brightened up.

"How long, boss?" one of them called, holding his bloody shoulder. "How long 'fore we get there?"

Sally Can't Dance had popped a disc into the boom box, and Lynyrd Skynyrd's "Sweet Home Alabama" filled the air.

Cyrus cupped his hands around his mouth and yelled: "Not long, friend! It won't be long now!"

FIFTEEN

The two tandem-seat Cobra attack helicopters roared over the desert at 190 miles per hour, Malloy in the front gunner's seat of one, Larkin in the other.

"We have visual contact, Vince," his pilot, Gator, said into his mike. "About five miles, ten o'clock."

Larkin scanned the sky off slightly to his left and saw the tiny form. "That was quick."

"A while back, looked like there was only one contrail. Maybe they lost an engine."

Malloy's voice came on. "Let's take 'em out, Larkin."

"We're not taking them out, Malloy. We're not killing everybody, if we don't have to."

"Don't be so lily-livered, Larkin."

"That is my plane. My men are in it. Right now it's my responsibility."

"Jesus, how prissy can you get!"

"You understand me, Malloy? You understand the command here?"

Malloy did not respond.

The music stopped. Cyrus stood by the boom box, his finger on the "off" button, and in his other hand the black Beretta automatic that once belonged to Agent Sims. All eyes fell on him as he started to stroll down the aisle, speaking slowly, distinctly, calmly.

"Now," he said, counting on his index finger, "first, someone alerted the authorities in Carson City. All of a sudden, the bulls had us pegged. Where'd that come from? And then, second, someone told them about the rendezvous at Lerner. How would anybody know we're coming down in Death Valley? Cindino knew, but even though he was double-crossing us, he wanted to get out of there without being discovered just as much as we did. Now, could these things be coincidence? Just bad luck? Maybe. Not likely, but maybe."

Cyrus reversed his course in the aisle and headed back up, scanning the eyes. "And then there's poor Billy Bedlam. Somebody offed that poor bastard. It ain't coincidence that tossed him up on a hook like an old coat. And back there at Lerner, somebody went and chained us to the ground just when we were about to take off. Who would do a thing like that? Would a friend do that? That ain't coincidence, tying us down like a damn mule."

He turned again and paced the other way, still examining faces. "So I ask you, what is going on? And I'll answer myself: We got a rat around."

Convicts looked at each other.

Cyrus nodded. "Yup. Somebody has turned, or been turned all along. And him who turned ain't one of the dudes we left on the ground back there filled with government bullets. Because Swamp Thing says we weren't chained down when he got on board to fire up and get us out of there. So whoever turned is right here in Con Air city."

Now the convicts avoided looking at each other and shifted their feet nervously.

"So how we flush him out?" Cyrus continued. "How we get the rat out of his hole? Well, you can set out something he wants. Or you can set out something he doesn't want."

Abruptly he turned and grabbed Guard Bishop in a headlock and stuck the gun barrel in her ear. "Let's count together: one . . ."

Nobody dared join the count. Bishop avoided Poe's eyes. Baby-O squirmed.

". . . two . . ."

Poe tensed to make a move, when Baby-O sang out:

"It was me!"

Heads whirled toward him.

"Me, bro's. I did it all."

Cyrus cocked his head, eyeing him. "You been near death the entire trip."

"Slick, huh?" Baby-O smiled. "I got all you guys going my way." He hugged himself and rocked forth and back, laughing strenuously. "I do declare, I never saw so many easy marks on one gummint plane in my entire crooked life! And I'm gettin' *paid* for it—can you imagine?"

"You ain't been paid by me, yet, bro," Cyrus said, softly, leaning over close. "We got a saying, the wages of sin is death." He put the gun to Baby-O's chest and fired once. He backed away casually as Baby-O doubled over.

Baby-O forced himself back upright. "How I look, bro?" he rasped to Poe who quickly bent over him.

"What the hell were you thinking, bro?" Poe whispered in his ear, hugging him gently.

"Tired of you hogging all the heroics, bro. Oh, man."

Poe opened Baby-O's shirt and felt delicately around to locate the wound under the blood. "I think you got lucky. Missed the heart, I think."

"I don't feel good, bro."

"Nobody would. I'm counting on you to hang on."

Baby-O nodded and closed his eyes, trying to relax and control his breathing.

Poe heard a little-girl's voice mimicked behind him:

" 'My daddy is coming home on July 14. My birthday is July 14. I am going to see my daddy for the first time ever on July 14. . . .' "

Poe looked up to see Cyrus, standing next to Diamond Dog near the floor hatch in the front of the cabin. He was holding Casey's crayon-written letter.

" '. . . I can't wait for July 14. . . .' "

"You slimy bastard. . . ." Poe coiled in his seat, ready to spring.

" '. . . Love, Casey.' " Then Cyrus was handed the pink bunny Diamond Dog had been holding behind his back. Cyrus held it up and stuck the gun in its ear. "Make a move, Cameron Poe, and the bunny gets it. Relax, Poe. You can't do anything." He tucked the bunny's arm under his belt so it dangled awkwardly, keeping his pistol trained now on Poe.

He took a step closer to Poe, sighting down the barrel. "Now, I have a choice. I can do you neat, like Baby-O, by planting the muzzle right on you.

Or I can do you sloppy, by blowing your head open from here. Maybe I'll give you the choice. Which you want, Cameron Poe? I'll bet you prefer tidy."

Suddenly Cyrus stiffened, seeing through the rear hatch the Cobra, just then rising into view at close range. He fired at it, the bullets whanging off the Cobra's windshield.

From the Cobra came a burst of answering machine-gun fire. Convicts dove for cover, seats exploded into foam-rubber snow. Cyrus belly flopped on the floor, his gun skittering toward the rear. He scrambled to all fours, raced forward, and dove toward a cage, where his head whacked a box and knocked him woozy.

"No, no!" Larkin hollered into his mike. "What the hell you doing?"

"He's firing at us, Vince," Gator said.

"It's a damn *pistol*, Gator!" Larkin railed. "This whole cockpit is only three feet wide—he's not gonna hit us again! You got *orders*!"

"Okay, okay." Gator swerved the chopper out of the line of fire, dropping below the C-123.

In the second Cobra, the Provider's position was tracked by computer and displayed on twin monitors. Cross hairs showed the exact point of aim for the thirty-millimeter cannon.

"Time to be a man, Larkin!" Malloy called from that Cobra. "Strap a hog on and let's start mixing it up!"

The pilot squeezed the trigger and fired a burst into the C-123.

As everyone else huddled behind and under the seats, Poe raced down the aisle and slammed the rear mesh door, closing off the rear half of the plane and about half the cons. He scooped up Cyrus's pistol.

He retreated quickly up the suddenly quieter cabin to drop into the seat beside Baby-O. He cradled the wounded man in his arms.

"I'm getting a bad feeling, bro," Baby-O said in a fainter voice. "I'm getting a feeling like I'm not gonna make it."

"Knock it off. You're gonna make it."

"Maybe I'm not *supposed* to make it."

"What the hell you mean by that?"

"Maybe I really *am* being punished for my sins."

"Bullshit. We'd all be sitting here gutshot."

Baby-O began to hic softly, and tears rolled down his cheeks. "All I can think about is like there ain't no Great Spirit up there, like they say. He don't exist. And that scares me, for when I die."

"You ain't dying, bro!" Poe got up.

"Where you going?"

"I'm gonna be your Great Spirit. You sit tight and watch."

Poe stomped up the aisle toward the cockpit.

Diamond Dog confronted him in the aisle, puffing out his chest. "Where you think you're going, white boy?"

He never saw Poe's left hook, and wouldn't remember it. He dropped to the floor like a bag of sand. Poe stepped over him. Conrad stepped up next, then Viking. After they crumpled, other cons gave way.

There was one more big mesh door between him and the cockpit. Poe slammed it behind him, closing off pursuit by anybody in the cabin.

Then he stepped into the cockpit.

Swamp Thing was moving the stick left and right, in what he knew were vain moves to shake the Cobras. He was flying a slow plane that was already down an engine. But his training and habit were to take evasive action.

Poe stuck the gun in his ear, causing Swamp Thing to jump and then freeze.

"You got fat nuts," Swamp Thing said, not moving a hair.

"I'm the new captain, pal."

"Malloy, you son of a bitch!" Larkin spouted. "Cease fire! You're violating a federal order!"

But Malloy's Cobra swung into position for what looked like a second attack.

"Gator! Get in his way!"

"What?"

"Get in his way, between him and the one twenty-three. He won't fire on us."

"You sure? He seems a bit unwrapped to me."

"Do it."

Gator sent the Cobra into a slanting dive in front of the other gunship.

"You stupid bastard!" Malloy radioed.

"Deal with it," Larkin answered. "You want a dogfight?"

"I got no move," Malloy's pilot radioed. "Your play."

"Settle down, then. Jesus Christ, we're both supposed to be working for the same U.S. of A.!"

SIXTEEN

"Cyrus Grissom! Cyrus? This is Vince Larkin. You got your ears on? I'm right behind you, loaded. Don't mess with me like that, pal. You there? How are you?"

Poe snatched the radio mike. "Hold your fire!"

"Who's talking?"

"Cameron Poe. Hold your fire."

"Give me a reason."

"I'm gonna bring her down. I got command here now. It's okay. We'll take her down easy. We're all yours."

"Malloy?" Larkin radioed. "You copy?"

"What now, you patsy?"

"Listen to him, Malloy. He's a friend, not an enemy." He heard what sounded like muted gunfire over the radio. "Poe? What you got there?"

"I sealed 'em off," Poe answered. "Sounds like they're firing at the door. Let's get this done."

In Malloy's Cobra, the pilot was concentrating on his ranging device. "I have target locked on, sir," he said. "Locked on for missile." He got no response from Malloy behind him. "Sir? We're not over civilian population at the current time. Now is good."

Malloy squirmed with indecision. Then he said, "Hold fire."

"Pardon?"

"I said, hold fire! Don't second-guess me. Lock off!"

"Roger, sir."

The altimeter dropped past 8,000 feet. The wings waggled. The plane shuddered.

Swamp Thing sighed. "We're out of juice, Poe. We just lost the second engine."

"Feather it. Land this thing."

"Oh, I'll feather the prop. And we'll go down, all right. But this ain't no glider, you know. We might not be recognizable after we plop into the sagebrush and spread ourselves over three Nevada counties."

The Provider dipped lower and lower. The

ground eased up toward them. At a thousand feet, the Cobras were still on their tail, but that wasn't of nearly as much interest to Poe and Swamp Thing as the prospect for a crash.

Poe heard the mesh door in the cabin give way. He ducked out of the cockpit to see Cyrus and others trying to wrench the door open. He flipped the lever to open the cages and free the hostage guards—they scurried for the seats to strap themselves in.

Poe met Cyrus head on outside the cockpit doorway.

"Say good night, Giantkiller," Cyrus snarled, leveling his gun at him once again, trying to steady himself against the yawing of the descending plane.

But bullets instead whanged off the walls near Cyrus; Bishop had picked up the pistol from the floor under Diamond Dog, and now she blew smoke off the barrel tip, smirking at the form of Cyrus covering his head on the floor.

Poe ducked back into the cockpit in time to see the lights of Las Vegas looming ahead of them.

"Nice sight," Swamp Thing said.

"Can they make it to the airport?" Larkin asked.

"No way," Gator answered. "Few years ago,

they might've made it to the desert. Vegas is too big now. It's gonna be a mess."

"You feel like some blackjack?" Larkin asked.

"Wonder what they feel like."

"Hey, Larkin," Malloy radioed. "We should've dropped it over the open desert, Larkin. Now you're looking at civilian population. That plane's headed for the middle of it."

"Thanks for calling my attention to it," Larkin said. He switched bands and put in an emergency call. ". . . Police, fire engines, ambulances—we're gonna need it all . . . I know you can't hear anything, because their damn engines are out! . . . I don't know just where, but it's gonna be damn close to downtown. There'll be a big, flat plane marking the spot. . . ."

The Provider sank below 500 feet, narrowly missing a water tower and broadcasting antenna, then an apartment complex. Pedestrians gawked in astonishment as the dark shape slid over their heads.

Cyrus burst into the cockpit. "You're dead, Cameron Poe," dancing to keep his feet as the plane shuddered with the landing gear down.

"We're all dead, Virus."

Garland Greene stood in the doorway, singing, ". . . He's got the little bitty baby in His hands. . . ."

Vegas World slid by underneath, the Riviera Hotel, and the water park at the Sahara. The fuselage vibrated violently as Swamp Thing wrestled with the flaps to keep the dying plane level.

The Provider clipped high-tension wires and bounced on Las Vegas Boulevard. It bounced again and again, the neon lights whizzing by, the one-hundred-ten-foot wings slapping a dozen parked cars. With a horrendous metallic screeching and grinding, the plane slid past the Stardust, the Desert Inn, Treasure Island—the last of which stripped off the wings. It broke into three sections as it came to a stop in the porte cochere of the Mirage Hotel.

For a long moment there seemed to be absolute silence within and without the dead transport. Then:

"You're dead, your little girl is dead, your bunny is dead!" Cyrus picked himself up off the floor and lunged for Poe, who was still on his knees.

Poe drove a fist up into Cyrus's groin before he was toppled over backward under the big man. Poe used the momentum to flip Cyrus on over so he landed on his back and lay stunned with the wind knocked out of him.

Poe scrambled up and headed for the main cabin in the broken fuselage.

Emergency vehicles and personnel swarmed the site, fire retardant flooded the plane from fixed nozzles atop fire trucks. Police raced around setting up a secure perimeter. Medical technicians grabbed their gear and edged toward the plane, unsure of whether it was about to blow or not.

Army and National Guard trucks arrived, uniformed men piled out with their rifles and took up firing positions. Prison officials and guards massed for an advance.

The Cobras landed behind the wreck, and Malloy and Larkin leaped out and ran for the C-123.

Through a split in the fuselage, Sally Can't Dance appeared, wide-eyed, stepping carefully, looking around at the lagoons and palm trees at the Mirage.

"We made it!" Sally yelled, with arms spread wide and high. "We made it to Cindino's Island!"

Poe passed cons still strapped in their seats, too dazed to move. Others, some bloodied from head bumps, extricated themselves and got to their wobbly feet. Empty seats were scattered all over. Smoke and dust roiled through the cabin.

Poe was bleeding from the top of his head—with no recollection of what he'd bounced off of when the plane hit the street. He wiped a stream of blood out of his eyes, so he could find Baby-O.

Baby-O lay supine on the floor between some seats. Blood now colored his entire shirt and the front of his pants. His face was bloodless, his skin clammy, his eyes fluttering.

"Hey, bro," Poe said, kneeling to take his hand. "How you doing?"

"Just fine, bro."

"Get a doctor in here!" Poe bellowed toward the crowd milling outside the split in the fuselage. "Get a doctor!"

"I'm cool, bro. I still get to come over for the barbecue?"

"Of course."

"Even though we didn't quite get to where we was supposed to get to finish up, right?"

"We got far enough, bro." Poe ripped off Baby-O's shirt and made a bandage of it to tie around his chest. "Don't know why I didn't do this before."

"You got busy, bro. You was off being the Great Spirit. You done good, Ranger man. But you're wasting your time now."

"What I do with my own time is none of your business. *Get a doctor in here, goddamn it!*"

Cons staggered off the plane into the arms of cops and prison guards. Sally Can't Dance, still crowing, was seized by both arms by officers.

"The name is Salvatore Candoza," she sang to the television cameras. "I'll be writing a book about this!"

A pair of emergency medical technicians climbed into the fuselage, hauling a gurney with them.

"Here! Here!" Poe yelled, waving them over.

"Tell me about that barbecue again, bro."

"Red-hot baby backs, burgers, bacon, grits, black-eyed peas, pinto beans, endless Bud outta the keg."

The EMTs carefully fitted the sling under him and hoisted him aboard the gurney.

"Gimme odds, bro," Baby-O said, reaching for Poe's extended hand.

"Shit, ain't no odds I'd cover on you." Poe spat onto the floor. "You're a sure bet. I'll see you later, when you're cleaned up."

They wheeled Baby-O out into the loud, boiling mass of cops, gamblers, television cameras, and all the others scrambling around the site. Poe followed right behind them.

"Hold it right there!" barked a cop with his gun drawn. Another officer quickly joined him.

Poe stopped and raised his hands.

"Easy, officer," Bishop called, stepping over some debris and holding her hand up. "That's a citizen there. I can vouch. Let him help his friend to the ambulance."

"We can't just—"

"He was my prisoner. Still is. Let him go."

Reluctantly, the officers stepped aside.

They slid Baby-O into the ambulance.

"What're you gonna do now?" Bishop asked Poe.

He looked at her. "I got a choice?"

"Far as I'm concerned."

"I started this day aiming for a birthday party. I'd still like to try for that. Thanks."

"Hey, thanks for my life, Poe."

"Well. . . ." He looked at the ground.

"Go ahead on, get outta here."

Larkin prowled through the dark and smoky innards of what had been a perfectly good C-123K Provider. "Where's Grissom?" he asked to anybody he passed.

Two paramedics were standing at the first cage, looking in. Johnny Twenty-Three was lying on the floor, a body now. His wrist was still cuffed to the cage, exposing the row of conquered hearts.

"You better take him away," Larkin said, unlocking the cuffs.

When they lifted the body, the arm stayed, severed completely, swaying with its heart tattoos.

Larkin stifled the urge to barf and continued searching through the plane. The few cons that were left were busted up and no threat to anybody. None of them was Cyrus "the Virus" Grissom. He groped his way back outside.

He found himself facing Cameron Poe, on the other side of the man-made "volcano" facsimile in front of the Mirage. As if on cue, the "volcano" erupted; the two were invisible to each other, separated by flames, steam, lava.

They both turned, and they both saw a lone fire truck roar to life and start to pull away. And as they watched, a black-coated fireman was thrown from the truck, to flop on the road and sit there rubbing his helmetless head.

"Grissom!" Larkin muttered, glimpsing his prey hanging to a handrail on the departing truck.

Poe saw Swamp Thing at the wheel of the truck and Conrad at the back, and then Diamond Dog clinging to the far side.

Larkin sprinted for the truck, leaping onto its rear and grabbing the rails, just as Swamp Thing activated the siren.

They went wailing down Las Vegas Boulevard, a heavy and slow-moving battering ram, scattering spectators, clipping cars and sending them spinning, snapping off an occasional light or sign.

Larkin pulled himself up on the rear handrails, seeing above him the grinning face of Cyrus the Virus. Larkin had an instant to notice the irony that he was still wearing his guard uniform.

"Welcome aboard!" Cyrus shouted. "But nobody rides for free!" He kicked Larkin in the face, knocking him loose from the rails and dislodging him from the truck.

Larkin picked himself up off the street just as Cameron Poe skidded to a stop beside him riding a state trooper Electra Glide motorcycle and motioned for him to jump on.

Larkin sprang onto the seat behind Poe and they set off after the fire truck that was still plowing up the avenue. Three state troopers on their own Electra Glides joined the pursuit, hitting their sirens. It sounded like an air raid.

Cyrus watched the bikes close on them. Diamond Dog climbed across to the pump-control panel and threw some switches. Cyrus clambered to the rear hose bed and hoisted a fat length of hose and yanked back the handle of the nozzle.

A mighty jet of water came at the bikes, twenty gallons a second at a force of 150 pounds per square inch, and one of the troopers was slapped off his bike as neatly as if severed from it by a scythe. Cyrus shifted to the second one and popped him off, then the third. He trained the stream then on the bike carrying Larkin and Poe.

Poe leaned to swerve away. "You packing?" he called back to Larkin.

"What?" Larkin strained to hear over the wind and water.

"You got a gun?"

"Yeah!"

"Shoot him with it before he kills somebody!"

Larkin extracted his pistol from his lower back, tried vainly to steady himself without holding on so he could aim with both hands, and fired in the general direction of Cyrus. Poe leaned and weaved to maneuver the bike around the jet of water. Larkin fired again and again, not sharp enough to hit Grissom, but close enough to make him drop the hose and scramble for safety back into the cab.

Poe cranked up the bike and pulled alongside the truck. Diamond Dog emerged and hung onto the side of the rig, wielding a six-foot pipe puller whose end was a fierce claw.

With his feet anchored behind flanges on the truck, again and again Dog jabbed at Poe. One of his thrusts took a healthy nip out of Poe's arm. On the last jab, Larkin grabbed the end of the pull and hooked the claw onto the motorcycle seat.

Diamond Dog, his feet firmly planted under the flanges on the truck and holding onto the rod as if it were a lifeline, was suddenly stretched out over the street like a banner.

"Take the wheel!" Poe yelled to Larkin.

Larkin grabbed the handlebars as Poe climbed from the bike onto the horizontally stretched form of the flying Diamond Dog and crawled up his length to the truck as if he were a gangplank. Once there he tried to kick Dog's feet free of the flanges.

Diamond Dog let loose of the pipe pull and managed to draw himself back erect on the truck and took two roundhouse swings at Poe, during the second of which Poe kicked Dog's feet out from under him. Diamond Dog did almost a complete

revolution before splatting on the pavement with
his head open like a dropped melon.

Cyrus came at Poe over the top of the rig, swinging an axe. Poe ducked and found his hands on a
crowbar. They went at it, axe to crowbar, like two
heavyweight fencers, while Larkin kept the motorcycle alongside.

Cyrus slapped away Poe's crowbar. Poe ducked
another swing and slid under the aerial ladder and
disappeared. Cyrus crawled after him, searching.

Suddenly Cyrus reared back in a freezing cloud
of carbon dioxide, and Poe appeared with the fire
extinguisher still spouting and crawled out on the
lowered aerial ladder. Cyrus tumbled over backward, regained his footing, and found the levers on
the turntable that operated the ladder.

He pulled a lever, and the ladder bearing Poe
began to extend outward. Poe scrambled back
along the ladder toward the base, but slower than
the ladder was extended out, so he was getting far-
ther away all the time. Cyrus worked the controls
until he managed to get the turntable turning,
swinging the ladder around.

Poe made one complete orbit of the truck, flailing to keep a grip, part of the time hanging from
the ladder a couple of feet off the pavement. The
truck careened, swinging him violently, until he
could pull himself back onto the rungs.

Cyrus got the ladder to reverse itself, to retract back in on the truck, where he waited to pounce.

Poe dropped off onto the rig and slipped away again, only to come up behind Cyrus and get an off-balance shot at him that clipped his shoulder. They both grappled for holds on the ladder. Poe caught a glimpse of the now riderless motorcycle headed for a palm tree.

Suddenly they were going up. The ladder was being extended with both Poe and Cyrus on it. Below them, Larkin, fresh from his leap from bike to truck, was working the controls.

They grasped and scratched at each other as the truck roared and veered under them and the ladder kept getting longer. Poe's fingers found a set of cuffs in the back pocket of Cyrus's guard uniform. He yanked them out, and in one motion clapped one cuff around Cyrus's free hand and the other around the rung of the ever-extending ladder.

"Poe!" Larkin was pointing furiously ahead of them.

Poe reversed his strategy instantly, disengaging and sliding down the ladder.

Cyrus, cuffed to the ladder rung, looked ahead to where Larkin was pointing and saw the highway overpass a few agonizing seconds before the ladder met it and the top half, including Cyrus, was chopped off in a hail of slivers and cables and gore.

The force of that split opened the truck tanks, and a Niagara of water exploded, and the truck veered into the abutment, sending Swamp Thing hurtling fatally into the windshield.

In a few dizzying moments, Larkin was lying on the ground having his head bandaged by a paramedic.

Malloy was crouching over him. "You okay?"

"Who wants to know?"

"Yeah, yeah, you got a right. But we got the job done."

"Yeah." As he turned his head to watch Malloy give the peace sign and walk away, he saw that Poe was lying beside him, having bandages applied to his arm. "Nice job, Poe."

"Strange team, huh?"

"Yeah."

The medics finished and the men got to their feet, both feeling a little dizzy and fully exhausted.

A police van pulled up, and Marshal Ginny Clark stepped out, cute as ever but with lines of worry now etched into her face. Behind her came Tricia, hand in hand with Casey.

Poe turned away and walked quickly over to the remains of the fire truck and rummaged around.

Larkin smiled and took Ginny's arm. "Come on, Marshal. I owe you a dinner."

"I'll serve you like a geisha," she said.

"That's not like you, to say something like that."

"No. Not like you to hear it, either."

They both laughed as they walked away, but quickly he winced and put his hand to his head. They resumed a quiet pace.

When Poe came back from the truck, he was carrying the pink bunny, now grease-stained, bloodstained, and one-armed.

Cops again stepped in front of him.

So did Malloy, but he faced the cops, not Poe. "What the hell are you doing?" he said. "Let the man see his family. I'm in charge here. I'm vouching for him."

"Okay, okay." The cops backed away, holding their palms up.

"Hello, Tricia," Poe said.

"Hello, Cameron."

"You look the same."

"So do you."

"Sorry. I've got a present." He knelt down in front of Casey. "This thing is a mess. But I been carrying it a long way, for a long time. Happy birthday."

"Thanks, Daddy." She took the bunny cautiously, then looked up at him. "This is the first time I've seen you, you know."

"I know."

"I love you," Tricia said.

They fell into an embrace, and Casey hugged his leg, and they both extended an arm to include her.

Larkin and Ginny strolled past the wreckage of the C-123, gaping at the tumult that still surrounded it.

"How were the peanuts?" Ginny asked.

He laughed gingerly. "You got plans for the weekend?"

"What, me?" She feigned surprise and put a hand to her chest. "Same old same old. Pizza and sports. You interested?"

"Yup."

"Mr. Larkin!" a cop called, trotting behind them. "Mr. Larkin, I found this." He handed him a plastic ID bracelet bearing the name "Garland Greene."

"Garland," Larkin mused. "He's still around."

"Killed thirty people?" Ginny asked.

"That's the guy. Ginny, meet me at the restaurant, okay? This will be quick, or I won't find anything at all."

"Sure."

He went into the casino and scanned the crowd. He wandered past the slots and wheels and settled at the craps table.

Chips were out. The stickman reached out with his stick to gather the dice and push them to the end. "New shooter coming out. New shooter. Feel lucky?"

The dice were picked up at the end.

"Hold it," Larkin said. "I'm in." He laid down a hundred-dollar bet. He looked at the man who picked up the dice. "Feeling lucky?"

The shy man in the ill-fitting suit smiled back sheepishly. "Kinda," he said. He rolled the dice.

"Snake eyes," Larkin called out before anybody else. "You got snake eyes, Garland Greene. You ready to come with me?"

Garland Greene shrugged. "Sure, why not?"